LOVE FINDS A WAY

Also by Lester Wertheimer

AT SEA
Being an Eccentric Voyage of Discovery
In the Company of Misfits, Rogues, and Vagabonds

IT COULD BE WORSE
Or How I Barely Survived My Youth

TRUE LOVES
My Fellowship Year Abroad

Love Finds a Way

A ROMANTIC NOVEL

Lester Wertheimer

LOVE FINDS A WAY
A Romantic Novel

This is a work of fiction. All of the characters, names, incidents, organizations, and dialogue in this novel are either the products of the author's imagination or are used fictitiously.

iUniverse books may be ordered through booksellers or by contacting:

iUniverse LLC
1663 Liberty Drive
Bloomington, IN 47403
www.iuniverse.com
1-800-Authors (1-800-288-4677)

ISBN: 978-1-4917-3342-4 (sc)
ISBN: 978-1-4917-3344-8 (hc)
ISBN: 978-1-4917-3343-1 (e)

Library of Congress Control Number: 2014908141

Printed in the United States of America.

iUniverse rev. date: 06/20/2014

For

Elyse Lewin

A modern-day goddess,

if there ever was one.

I ran into Isosceles the other day.
He has a great idea for a triangle.

Woody Allen

ONE

"You are *such* an idiot," growled Lisa, "you make every other idiot on earth look like Albert Einstein." She was responding to something I just said, and though I might have chosen better words, I can assure you it was not idiotic. You should know that Lisa, my beloved wife for the past six years, wasn't always the pain in the neck she now appeared. In fact, when we first got together I thought she was perfect in every way. I mean *every* way. She was bright, talented, and with a figure that caused men to stare and women to go green with envy. Lisa had that rare combination of looks—a fair complexion, dark hair, and pale blue eyes. It was an unusual blend of features that made her—in my opinion—the loveliest creature on earth. But it was her personality that really charmed me. She was an optimist with a ready smile and a disposition as sweet and appealing as a hot fudge sundae.

But that was a lifetime ago, and now everything was different. Lisa and I had hit a bump in the road that would have stopped an armored tank dead in its tracks. That remark about me being the idiot who would make all other idiots look like a genius was not the first time she suggested I was uniquely deficient. I had been called, among other unprintable terms, a fool, moron, birdbrain, nincompoop, imbecile, jackass, and shmuck. When it came to insults Lisa was an unrestrained, fire-breathing thesaurus. And when she wasn't hurling nasty epithets she often dropped the dreaded "D" bomb. "That's it George; dammit,

I want a divorce. I don't like you, and I want you out of here." A day or so later she invariably had a change of heart. I suppose keeping me around to endure her abuse was preferable to separating. Clearly, our once perfect marriage was on life support, and what remained of our relationship was eroding faster than the polar ice cap.

Though I knew it was foolish to continue the conversation I could not let it go. "Why then," I asked sarcastically, "did you choose to marry an idiot?"

"Who knows? I might have been drunk. Yes, that was it; I was drunk."

That was not it; she was not drunk. We were married because we loved one another, but that was long ago. These days, we often didn't speak, because a misunderstood word or two would often result in an endless argument. It was simply easier to live as two contentious roommates, remote and miserable.

Later that evening, as she crawled into bed, she asked, "What were we arguing about?" Strangely, neither of us could recall the focus of the dispute. So that's what it's come to, I thought; our quarrels are so meaningless they're not even worth remembering. I pulled back the covers, got into bed, and turned out the light. Our bodies were as far apart as our king-sized bed allowed.

We lay there silently until Lisa said, "I think we should get away."

"From each other?" I asked.

"Not a bad idea, but I was thinking maybe we should get away from it all, take a trip, and see if there's anything here worth saving. You know, I'm not very happy."

"That's pretty obvious. Have you considered a trip to your psychiatrist?"

"Don't be nasty; our problem involves us both, and we ought to work on this together. I think we need something like a cruise. I've been thinking a lot about that lately. I hear the Greek islands are loaded with history and very romantic."

"I hate the idea of cruising," I said. "Why would you want to be surrounded by old people boring you to death with stories of their exceptional grandchildren? I can think of so many less painful ways to be unhappy."

"Why are you always so negative?"

"I'm not always negative; it's just that cruising is not my thing. Frankly, if I'm going to be miserable, I'd rather stay home."

"Okay, forget the cruise," she said disconsolately. "What if we *flew* to Greece?"

"Lisa, do you really think traveling seven thousand miles will change anything? Do you believe marriages *can* change? Would being in Greece suddenly encourage us to hold hands again, or God forbid, be civil to one another?"

"I don't know," she said, "I really don't know. But staying here and doing nothing will surely be the end of us." She seemed at that moment as deeply depressed as I'd ever seen her. But I knew she was right; if we didn't try something different, we were certainly heading off a cliff.

"Let me sleep on that," I said. "We'll talk in the morning."

In fact, I slept little that night. Our endless quarrelling had not only damaged our affection for one another, but it made a good night's sleep nearly impossible. I wasn't sure how much longer this could go on. As I stared at the ceiling the familiar movie of our life began running in my mind. I'd seen this movie many times before, but never had I watched it with greater feelings of remorse.

The opening scene was always the same—the day we first met. It was a few months after I established my architectural practice, and there was Lisa, appearing like an absolute vision. Our encounter, however, was not especially promising. Let me rephrase that; our first encounter was a disaster. My client, a Bay Area entrepreneur, had hired a designer to develop interiors for my first commercial project. Unfortunately, he neglected to tell me about it. When I discovered that another person would be working on *my* creation, I was ready to do battle with whoever showed up. Lisa was the one who showed up, and worse yet, she brought along sketches of proposed modifications to my design. It was loathing at first sight.

"I hope you don't mind my making a few suggestions," she said sweetly, "but I think these ideas will improve your clever design."

I could hardly contain my annoyance. "As a matter of fact, I do resent your messing with my project. I've spent a lot of time on this, and every line is there for a reason. Nothing on these plans is arbitrary or—in my opinion—needs to be changed."

"Are you saying that your design is so perfect it cannot be improved?"

"I'm saying that everything here reflects my best design judgment."

"In *my* opinion, if you don't mind my saying, you're being a bit arrogant."

"I don't mind your saying, but I really have no interest in your opinion."

"Why are you being so narrow-minded," she asked. "Why not consider my ideas before rejecting them outright. And, by the way, why are you acting so nasty about this?"

"Look, I'm sorry we disagree, but this project is important to me. I also happen to think that no good design has ever been improved by committee thinking."

"I'm not a committee; I'm just someone who's trying to help. You don't have to be a bully, you know, I'm only trying to do the job I was hired to do. Like it or not, I have no intention of quitting, so I suggest you get used to the idea of having me around."

ONE

I wondered why this annoying creature had suddenly dropped into my life. I was getting along very well before she appeared, and I certainly didn't need anyone to gum up the works.

"I'm going now," she said. "I suggest we get together another time when you can act more rationally and less like a horse's ass."

And that's the way our first meeting went. Lisa walked out of the office, and I was forced to accept the fact that, one way or another, an interior designer would be part of my team. That being the case, I figured—what the hell—why shouldn't it be a stunning young woman? I also realized that my hostility should have been directed at our client, not the interior designer he selected behind my back. But I figured any confrontation with him would have resulted in both of us losing the job.

It was clear from the start that Lisa had remarkable talent and was then, as she remains today, the most attractive, charming, and extraordinarily desirable woman I ever knew. When we met, she was seeing a middle-aged film director who was an absolute cliché— successful, handsome, and, of course, filthy rich. He lived with his wife in a large house in Beverly Hills and drove a vintage Bentley. He apparently had it all—success, fame, and an immensely attractive mistress.

I, on the other hand, was the antithesis of the boyfriend. I was presentable, but with little success up to that point and just barely out of debt. My earnings paid the office expenses, with enough left over to fund a modest, but satisfactory, social life. I had an unpretentious apartment in Westwood and got around in a convertible Audi TT, my only real extravagance.

Lisa and I eventually learned to get along, and finally we became— if not friends—friendlier. We often lunched together, which gave us the opportunity to discuss our project and exchange thoughts about our lives. It was all quite amiable and without the slightest hint of romance. I became her confidant and heard much about her relationship, including the part about the director leaving his wife and the two of them flying off into the sunset. That notion first surfaced months before she and I met, and so far, remained an unfulfilled promise.

"It's not likely to happen," I would say. "He's got it working perfectly. Why would he upset his life, threaten his career, and sign on for a lifetime of alimony? He's only using you."

"You don't understand," she would answer. "He loves me."

"Do you love him?"

"He says he can't live without me," she would answer, avoiding my question.

"What he can't live without," I finally said, "is every expensive plaything in his toy chest, including a vintage Bentley and a star-struck, extramarital playmate. If his ego were any more inflated it would pop like a cheap balloon."

That was the part that made her cry. "You didn't have to say that. That really hurt."

"I'm sorry, Lisa; I like you, and I hate to see you marching off the cliff like a lemming."

We didn't speak for several days, but a week later we flew to San Francisco for a meeting with our client. We checked into a small hotel near Fisherman's Wharf and later had a wonderful dinner of freshly caught crab. It felt as though things were back to normal between us. She accepted my apology for our disagreement and even laughed when I made a joke about it. Later that evening I heard a knock on my door, and suddenly, there she was, looking absolutely stunning in a short skirt, hair kind of messy, and a perfume I found irresistible.

"Do you have a minute to go over some drawings?" she asked.

We spread out the papers on the desk, and I stood behind her as she sketched her proposed modifications over the plans. I tried to follow her thinking but found my mind filled with alien thoughts. Whether it was the dress, the perfume, or the situation I don't know, but I was simply unable to concentrate. Then she turned around and asked, "Well, what do you think?"

I was silent for a long time, until she asked, "George, have you been listening? I asked what do you think?"

I stared into her blue eyes and said, "No, I'm sorry, I didn't hear a word you said."

"What's wrong? Why are you staring at me like that?

"You asked what I think? Well, let me tell you what I think. I think you are the most desirable creature I've ever met, and I'm absolutely crazy about you. That's what I think."

Then I kissed her. It surprised us both, because it was completely spontaneous, and yet, the most marvelous moment I could ever have imagined. She kissed me back, and the temperature in the room rose several degrees. Within minutes we forgot about the job, forgot about the boyfriend, forgot about everything else, and ended up in a loving embrace. I knew then, without the slightest doubt, I had found the love of my life.

That night became a night to remember, and as my mental movie rolled on I recalled each detail and every nuance of our first encounter. We made love all night, and it felt as natural and wonderful as if we were the only two people on earth, as if we were actually Adam and Eve. I don't think we had more than three hour's sleep. At about four in the morning we walked to a nearby 24-hour coffee shop. When we finished eating we went back to bed and into each other's arms. Six months later, six of the most romantic months imaginable, we married, and there was no question, it was forever.

In those first years we were so crazy in love I could hardly believe my good fortune. Each month during our first year together I sent her a thank you card for being my wife. Honest to God, I thought she was absolute perfection. But I should have known that anything that wonderful couldn't possibly last. And, in fact, it didn't. Joy turned to sorrow, and that idyllic relationship became—almost overnight—a living nightmare. I kept wondering how that happened.

As my sleepless night continued, so did the movie of our life. There was a flashback to a medical office two years ago. We were surrounded by the usual wall-hung degrees and commendations that proved, beyond any doubt, the distinguished obstetrician sitting across from us was the most skillful practitioner on earth. The doctor was calm and almost apologetic as he informed us that we were unlikely to ever conceive a child. "Apparently," he said to me, "your sperm is defective." I had what he called *asthenospermia*, which sounds near fatal, but is relatively harmless. Asthenospermia is a condition in which one's sperm has poor movement. I had plenty of ammunition, so to speak, but my guys moved slowly and not always in a straight line. Who knew such a condition even existed? I tried several therapies over the next few months, but none of them worked. My sperm remained indifferent; those disoriented cells moseyed along like retarded slugs with no sense of direction.

One of Lisa's lifelong dreams was being a mother, and suddenly that was no longer an option. I suggested adoption, even a surrogate, but she would have none of that. "If we can't do it the normal way," she said, "we won't do it at all." And that was pretty much the beginning of the end. Lisa experienced a metamorphosis so swift my head was still spinning. She fell into a deep depression, became profoundly unhappy, and heaped the majority of her anger and abuse on her loving husband. In record time she went from classic angel to classic shrew. Oddly, I still loved her, but she was no longer easy to love; and sadly, my reservoir of patience was dangerously close to empty.

ONE

The final scene in the movie of our life was a fantasy straight out of a Hollywood musical. Lisa and I were waltzing through the Place de la Concorde, two Americans in Paris, oblivious to all and crazy in love. We stopped beside the classical fountain, embraced, kissed, and then continued our joyous dance. Our hearts were overflowing with love, and I knew then my blissful dream foretold a happier future. I was certain we would overcome all our problems and be blessed with everlasting love for the rest of our lives. It was the happiest of all possible Hollywood endings.

My eyes closed, the movie in my head faded to black, and finally, I drifted into a deep sleep.

The next morning Lisa asked, "So what do you think?"

"About what?

"Don't tell me you already forgot what we were talking about last night."

"Oh that. No I haven't forgotten. My first reaction was that quarreling in a different time zone would be pointless. But on second thought I figured a trip to Greece might be interesting and maybe even fun. So, what the hell, let's take a chance on our future. Let's go to Greece!"

Lisa smiled for what seemed the first time in a month, and that nearly made me forget the anxiety I felt that we were heading straight for the proverbial Bermuda Triangle.

TWO

Three weeks after we decided to visit Greece we headed to the airport for an overnight British Airways flight to London. As we left the house Lisa remarked, "Seriously, are you going to England looking like that?" I was wearing khaki pants, a plain white shirt, navy windbreaker, and loafers.

"Like what? I'm spending all night on a plane; I want to be comfortable."

"Whatever happened to your sense of dignity?"

"Now stop that, Lisa; this is hardly the way to begin a romantic adventure. I'm perfectly presentable and you're just being picky."

Lisa regarded the word "picky" as a shot across her bow. That resulted in the well-established pattern of her ignoring me for the first two hours of our flight. Eight more hours in the air, two ample meals, and one dreary movie later we landed at Heathrow. It was noon, but it felt like the middle of the night, which it actually was in California. We had reserved a riverfront room for two nights at the Savoy Hotel, and following that we would fly directly to Athens. Once there we would spend a week at the 140-year-old Hotel Grande Bretagne. Years earlier, as an architecture student, I visited Greece. In those days I stayed in youth hostels, but I swore that one day I would return and stay at the Grande Bretagne. It was elegant, stately, and within walking distance of the old city, the Acropolis, and other popular sights.

TWO

Our two days in London were better than I dared imagine. Lisa complained less than normal, if you don't count the reservation screw-up at Simpson's in The Strand. Our concierge had made our dinner reservation for the wrong time, so when we arrived there were no available tables. Lisa gave her best impression of an ugly American on holiday, and within ten minutes an empty table miraculously appeared. One would have thought that by this time I was beyond embarrassment, but I found myself apologizing to our waiter. "Please forgive my wife's outburst," I said. "She's suffering from jet lag and is really not herself."

"I completely understand," he replied, somehow sensing that his tip would reflect the full extent of my remorse.

Lisa ordered Dover sole, and I opted for the steak and kidney pie.

"You know," she said, "eating kidneys is disgusting."

"Then you should avoid them," I replied.

"How can I when they're sitting right across the table from me?"

"Lisa, please relax. I don't tell you what to eat, and you shouldn't tell me either."

My God, I thought, is there no end to her carping? It was like living with the world's strictest mother superior.

Our dinner was perfectly prepared and so delicious that by the time the dessert trolley rolled by, Lisa appeared to be, once again, the most delightful and rational person on the planet. Her mood swings were astounding.

During our two days in London we visited the National Gallery, St. Paul's Cathedral, and several popular monuments and parks. We also went window-shopping along Regent Street, while enjoying the unusually fair weather. I can recall only one awkward quarrel, and that began when a salesperson was unable to accept a credit card for a scarf Lisa wanted to purchase. My aggressive wife became so abusive to the poor salesgirl I was forced to intervene.

"Let me pay for it in cash," I said.

"Don't tell me you're taking the side of this young twit instead of supporting your wife."

"This is not a matter of taking sides, they just don't accept credit cards here. You're being unreasonable. I'll pay in cash; it's no big deal."

"Here we are," she snarled, "thousands of miles from home and nothing has changed; you're still acting like a pompous ass."

But she was wrong; something did change. A few hours later, as we were having dinner, Lisa apologized for her outburst that afternoon. It was a small gesture, but definitely a positive sign.

Early the next morning we caught our flight to Athens. We arrived in mid-afternoon, and as we stepped outside the terminal I noticed the mysterious glow of light that I recalled from my trip years earlier. There was a soft luminosity, unique to this part of the world that suffused the entire landscape. It was beautiful and curiously comforting.

After collecting our luggage we discovered that our transportation choice to the city was bus, taxi, or limo service.

"Let's go first class," I suggested.

"Why not?" she answered. "For all we know, this may be our last trip." An agent led us to a line of limousines and opened the door of the one at the head of the line.

"Do you speak English?" I asked.

"Yes, of course," answered the driver. "Where do you wish to go?"

"Do you know the Grande Bretagne Hotel?"

"Everybody knows the Grande Bretagne."

We drove off and headed for Constitution Square in downtown Athens. Our driver was tall, slender, and with a ready smile. His most distinctive feature, however, was his full head of dark hair. It was so abundant it appeared he was wearing a black fur hat, like a Russian in winter.

"What is your name?" I asked.

"Alexandros," he replied. "It means *Defender of Men*."

"That reminds me of Alexander the Great," said Lisa.

"Yes, he was a relative," said Alexandros. Then after a pause, "Is this you first trip to Greece?"

"I was here as a student," I answered, "many years ago."

"Quite a bit has changed. Quite a bit," he said strangely. "You will see."

I looked at Lisa, who shrugged as if to say, "What's that about?"

We had been driving for about twenty minutes when the car suddenly stopped. We were passing through an austere, rock-strewn area and before us was a small hill.

"Why are we stopped?" I asked.

"I cannot go any further," said Alexandros.

"What are you talking about? We need to get to our hotel."

"If you walk a few meters, just over that hill you will find someone who will take you where you wish to go. Trust me, it will be all right."

"This is crazy," said Lisa. "Why can't you take us into the city?"

"It is impossible. Please get out of the car now."

"We're not getting out until you explain what's going on." I was becoming confused and angry. What was beyond the hill? Were we walking into a trap? What the hell was going on? Alexandros removed the key from the ignition, got out of the car, and began to walk back towards the airport. He was deserting us, and we were being left to solve the mystery of our predicament.

Lisa looked stunned. "George!" she cried. "Do something!" I jumped out of the car and yelled at our disappearing driver. "Alexandros, come back here! I thought you were the defender of men. Come back here, you miserable fraud!" If he heard me he didn't acknowledge it. Now what were we supposed to do? I looked around but hadn't the faintest idea what was going on.

"Use your phone," said Lisa. "Call someone—anyone—the limo service, the auto club, the police!" I got out my cell phone and turned it on, but after a few moments I realized there was no signal. We were in one of those dead spots where phone service was simply unavailable.

"Sorry, there's no service out here. I think our only choice is to see what's over the hill." I got our bags and began the short walk. In a matter of minutes we reached the top of the hill and suddenly saw before us the city of Athens. But it looked different from what I remembered—more tidy and much smaller. Sitting under a nearby tree was a small cart hitched to a donkey. The driver of the cart was an old man with a bushy white moustache. He was dressed in a short, white tunic and wore a wide-brimmed straw hat.

"I've been waiting for you," he said in perfect English. It was incredibly weird, since his high-pitched voice and diminutive stature was reminiscent of a Munchkin from the Land of Oz.

"How did you know we'd be here? And, by the way, who *are* you?"

"My name is Doros; I am here to take you to the city." This dream was getting crazier by the minute; nothing made any sense.

"Tell me, Doros, do you know the way to the Grande Bretagne Hotel?"

"I'm sorry, sir, I have not heard of such a place. But I will take you to a comfortable inn where visitors often stay. I am sure you will like it."

"George," asked Lisa, "what the hell is going on? I'm getting very spooked by all this."

"I wish I knew. But what I do know is this: if we don't go with Doros, we have to walk."

We put our bags into the cart, sat on the narrow plank at the rear, and the donkey began to move. The unpaved path was rough, and we were soon swaying with every rut and pothole. After a short distance the road became smoother, and the donkey began to trot. I noticed footprints in the road, as well as tracings of other wheels. I also noticed a few people walking along the side of the road. All of them were dressed in loose tunics, much like Doros was wearing.

"Is there a festival going on, Doros? Everyone appears to be dressed for a celebration."

"There is always a festival for one god or another," he answered, "but I don't know of anything special happening today." What did he mean—*one god or another*?

"Maybe they're making a movie," said Lisa. "Is there a film crew in town, Doros?"

"A film crew? What is that?" This was fast becoming the Twilight Zone.

Suddenly I caught a glimpse of the Acropolis in the distance. I could almost hear my heart beating faster and the hair on my arms began to tingle. There was the Parthenon, the most prominent ancient temple in Greek history. There it was, boldly standing in all its perfection, but it was not the famous ruin I saw years before. This building appeared as though construction was just completed. Nothing was missing; it had its roof, walls, and even from a distance I could see that the famous missing sculptures, including the Elgin Marbles, were back in their proper place.

Then it struck me! As incredible as it appeared, and as astonishing as it sounded, there was no doubt we were actually in *ancient* Greece! There was no other rational explanation, not that this revelation was even remotely reasonable. We had somehow transmigrated more than twenty-five hundred years back in time! I sat quietly for a moment trying to decide how to break this extraordinary news to my unstable wife. I was sure she would see this as a malicious plot to drive her insane.

"Lisa," I began, "there's something odd going on here, something I can't explain or even begin to understand. But I think I know, at the very least, where we are. This is going to sound crazy, but just try to accept it."

"What are you trying to say?" she asked nervously.

"I'm pretty sure we're in *ancient* Athens. What I mean is, Athens as it was more than two thousand years ago." She sat quietly for a moment as my words sank in. Then she got an infuriated expression on her face, an expression I knew all too well.

"Do you think that's funny, George? Is that what you think? Don't you have anything better to do than make up bizarre stories to annoy me and make me even more anxious? You're not funny, George, you're sick; and this is hardly the time for a sick joke."

"This is no joke; honest to God, there's no other explanation. Look at the Parthenon; it's been in ruins for hundreds of years, and now it's perfect, all in one piece. Look at how people are dressed; everyone's wearing a tunic or a toga, and it's not even Halloween. Athens is a city of ten million people; where do you suppose they're hiding? Do you see any cars, any buses or streetcars—even a goddamn McDonalds? If this isn't ancient Greece, then what the hell is it?"

"Doros," Lisa asked our driver, "what year is this?"

"I'm not really certain," he began, "but next year will be the ninety-fourth Olympic cycle; each cycle, you know, consists of four years."

"Yes, but in what year was the first Olympic cycle?"

"Oh, I have no idea. Most people don't pay much attention to the passing years."

"Well, maybe," I interrupted, "you remember when the Parthenon was completed."

"I guess that was almost two years ago."

I remembered from Arch History that the Parthenon was completed in 432 B.C. So if I'm right, this year must be about 430 B.C. How incredible was that?

"I'm pretty sure, Lisa, this year is 430 B.C."

She sat quietly, apparently dazed by the news. Finally she said, "I refuse to believe that. This sort of thing just doesn't happen. Fairy tales aren't real, neither are Greek myths, and there's no such thing as a time machine. There has to be a rational explanation."

But I could not imagine what that explanation could be. This was ancient Greece, the year was 430 B.C., and until we awoke from this astonishing dream, we simply had to deal with it.

THREE

As Doros guided our cart towards the center of town we began to see more people, several other donkey carts, and a few herds of goats. Except for our bizarre predicament I rather enjoyed the journey. It was like watching an ancient Greek travelogue. Lisa sat quietly, appearing more confused and angry than entertained.

"How are you doing?" I asked.

"If you had anything to do with this, George, I swear to God I'll never forgive you."

"Lisa, believe me, I'm as totally bewildered as you."

We soon arrived at the Agora, which was an immense open space surrounded by temples dedicated to Olympian gods, workshops for craftsmen, and stalls for merchants. The area was mostly paved, but trees were planted along one side, and many people sat beneath them in animated conversation. There were also several statues of gods and statesmen scattered about, as well as public fountains that provided drinking water.

I remembered from school that the Agora was the principal marketplace, meeting place, and center of Athenian government. And, in fact, today it was lively and bustling, as people conducted their business or simply strolled about.

"This is the center of Athens," said Doros. "It is the most popular area of our city. Fortunately, it is close to where you are staying." He guided our cart along the edge of the Agora, turned right, and stopped several yards down the road in front of an attractive one-story structure.

"We are here," said Doros. Oddly, there was no sign or any other way to identify the place as an inn. In fact, the exterior stuccoed walls were featureless, except for a large wooden entrance door. Our driver carried our bags into an attractive, paved courtyard that featured several mature olive trees. A woman we assumed to be the proprietress approached and said, "Welcome to our inn, my name is Zoe. We have been expecting you." Zoe appeared to be in her early thirties. She was tall, slender, and wore a full-length tunic enhanced by an intricate silver necklace.

Suddenly, my frustration erupted. "How could you possibly be expecting us?" I asked. "We didn't make a reservation here, we have no idea where we are, and we don't know *you*." She stared at me with a completely blank expression. "And one more thing, can you explain why everyone here is speaking English?"

She looked particularly puzzled as she said, "I don't know what that is. We are speaking Greek . . . and so are you."

Lisa put into words what I was thinking. "God help us; we are losing our minds!"

"Follow me," said Zoe, "I will show you to your room." We walked across the courtyard and entered a small sitting room. Beyond the sitting room was a bedchamber, which was a modest space illuminated by one small window. The furnishings in both rooms were sparse and simply designed. I noticed that the bed was shorter and considerably narrower than our bed at home, and the mattress was composed of tightly woven sacks filled with—as I soon discovered—dried leaves. I decided to allow Lisa to discover that for herself. I wasn't in the mood for another melodramatic eruption.

"Where is the toilet?" asked Lisa.

"Come, I will show you," said Zoe.

The two women went off together, and I sat down in our small sitting room. A few minutes later Lisa came running in and gasped, "We cannot possibly stay here! The toilet is disgusting! It's the most primitive, dreadful thing I've ever seen! Nothing but a hole in a slab of stone, and no running water. Worse yet, there's no toilet paper! Just stones and leaves! I had to use my Kleenex!"

"Calm down; that's apparently the ancient way of doing things. I doubt if there's much we can do about that. As a matter of fact, flush toilets won't be invented for another two thousand years; and toilet paper, maybe a hundred years after that." Then my distraught wife—appearing totally defeated—began to cry. Her shoulders hunched forward, and her head sank to her chest.

"I don't know what I did to deserve this," she sobbed, "but was it so horrible that I was sent back in time two thousand years? Did you create this nightmare just to punish me?"

"Please understand—I had nothing to do with this. I don't know how or why we're in ancient Greece, and I have no idea when or *if* we'll get out of here. But we have to make the best of it. Let's just do what everyone else is doing. It will be like roughing it on a camping trip. If you need a trip to the toilet, it will be like taking a hike in the woods."

Lisa stopped crying, wiped her teary eyes, and finally said, "I know you blame me; I'm the one who wanted to go to Greece. I thought maybe things between us would improve, but now everything is so much worse."

"Neither of us is to blame for any of this. What's going on is way beyond blame."

Zoe interrupted, "You've been traveling a long time. Perhaps a bath would be calming. I will tell the help to assist you. I'm sure you will feel better after you bathe." She led us to a room off the courtyard that contained a large pool of steaming water. Standing by to serve us were two young women dressed in short togas.

"Allow the maidens to take care of you," said Zoe. "And please remove those strange garments you're wearing. I will bring you tunics and sandals." It was obvious she had little appreciation for the finest Saks Fifth Avenue and Brooks Brothers had to offer.

We did as we were told, a bit self-consciously I admit, and soon we were totally naked. As we entered the soothing water I glanced at Lisa's stunning figure and said, "For what it's worth, I still find you extraordinarily attractive."

"Thank you; but are you sure it's not the help that has aroused you?"

"I don't think so, Lisa, I really think it's you."

The maidens began to scrub away our anxiety and fatigue, and for the first time since our plane landed I began to relax. After soaking another twenty minutes we were directed to lie on smooth marble slabs while our attendants massaged our bodies with sweetly scented olive oil. The treatment went on for nearly an hour, during which I dozed for several minutes. It was the most thoroughly relaxing experience one could imagine, and even Lisa agreed. "Things are looking a bit less bleak," she murmured.

We put on our short tunics and sandals and were directed to a dining area where a modest feast was laid out. "Please help yourself," said Zoe, "and if you need anything just ask Polona and Thea, the maidens who bathed you earlier. They will be your slaves for as long as you are with us."

"Slaves?" I asked. "What do you mean? Do people actually own other people in Athens?"

"But of course; slavery is natural and necessary. Except for the poorest citizens, everyone has slaves. They represent a third of our population. Slaves are well treated, they are paid for their work, and one day they may purchase their freedom. Polona and Thea are sisters, and they are quite happy doing the work they do. Incidentally, Doros, the driver who brought you here, is also a slave."

"Who owns these people?" I asked.

"I do," she said nonchalantly.

Stretched across the table before us were platters of dried fish, cheeses, fruits, olives, and jugs of red wine. We had not eaten for what felt like a month, so our first meal in ancient Greece promised to be a memorable treat.

"Do you suppose this food is organic?" asked Lisa.

"What?" I asked. "Is that a joke?"

"No, I really care. You know I prefer eating organic."

"Listen carefully, Lisa; chemical fertilizers and pesticides won't be invented for another twenty-odd centuries. Everything here is organic! Good God! Everything!"

"Well you don't have to bite my head off."

"Sorry, I just think we have more to worry about than whether the food's organic."

A bit later Lisa said, "This is delicious, and by the way, can we afford this experience?"

"I have no idea. No one has mentioned money, and if they did I wouldn't know what to do. All we have are dollars, a few pounds, euros, and some credit cards. I'd be shocked if they accepted any of those."

"We might consider bartering," suggested Lisa. "My Kleenex alone should be worth a fortune." She was making a small joke; and, for the first time in a long time, she smiled.

According to my watch, which was still set on Los Angeles time, it was now noon, which meant it was ten in the evening in Athens. Fighting jet lag and exhausted from our bizarre adventure our eyes were beginning to close. "I've got to sleep," said Lisa, "I'm beat." We went to our room, took off our sandals and decided to sleep in our tunics. The idea of unpacking was simply too challenging.

"Do you think this mystery will ever be solved?" asked Lisa. "I must admit it's the strangest experience I've ever had."

"I don't really know. But here's what I suggest: let's have a time-out and stop quarreling. Supporting each other now may be the only way to avoid full-blown insanity. We need to put the past aside and try to muddle through together."

"I'll try," she said, "but I'm still dealing with a lot of heavy baggage."

We got into our narrow bed and tried to get comfortable lying on the sacks of dried leaves.

"You're right," said Lisa, "it's pretty much like camping out."

"This bed's fairly small," I said, "so if I bump into you during the night just ignore me."

"I don't mind a bump, but I'm not ready for much more."

"Who said anything about that? If I get horny during the night I'll just call for Polona or Thea—or maybe both. Sure, why not? They're our slaves."

"You wouldn't dare."

"Of course I would. And by the same token you can have Doros."

"Doros? He's old, bald, and a foot and a half shorter than I am."

"Yes, but for all you know, he may be the greatest lover in Athens."

"Why are we arguing about this nonsense?" she asked. "This will never happen."

"I suppose we're more comfortable arguing. It's the way we communicate." Ten minutes later we were both in a deep sleep.

I don't know when it was, but perhaps an hour later I felt Lisa touching my arm.

"Don't tell me you changed you mind. What a lovely surprise."

"This is not a joke," she replied. "I think someone's in our sitting room."

I was suddenly wide-awake, and every nerve tingled with the flow of adrenaline. I reached for my small travel flashlight, got out of bed, and cautiously walked into the sitting room.

I switched on the light and the powerful light-emitting-diode beam forced our intruder to cover his eyes. "Holy mother of Zeus!" he cried, "It's Helios, god of the sun! Spare me your powerful light; I am here on a peaceful mission."

I turned out the light and lit an oil lamp. I noticed our visitor was a handsome young man who was naked from the waist up, with only a short piece of fabric covering his lower body. He wore a cap with small wings and sandals that also had small wings.

"Who the hell are you?" I asked. "And what are you doing in our room?"

"I am Hermes," he replied "I dwell on Mount Olympus, and I've come to do my father's bidding."

"What are you talking about? Who is your father?"

"My father is Zeus, ruler of Mount Olympus and king of all gods." I figured he was either drunk, a lunatic, or our incredible nightmare had just morphed into a super-Olympian gear.

"What do you want with us?"

"Are you familiar with *filoxenia*?" he asked. Noting my blank stare, he continued. "Filoxenia is a love of strangers, a generosity of spirit, and a defining attribute of our people. It began years ago when my father often disguised himself by dressing in rags and visited Greek homes to learn how people treated strangers. Later he would reveal himself as a god. That is how people were encouraged to treat foreigners with kindness, because they never knew if they were dealing with a god in disguise."

By this time Lisa had joined us and, by the look on her face, appeared to be as astonished as I by what she heard.

"So you came by just to see if we were being treated well?" she asked.

"Yes," replied Hermes. "Aside from being messenger of the gods, I am also guardian of wayfarers and patron of orators, poets, and athletes."

"You're a pretty busy guy," I said. "But what are you doing here in the middle of the night?"

"My life is hectic, as you can imagine. I've already been to Sparta, Corinth, Delphi, and the island of Melos today. Please excuse the lateness of my visit."

"Not a problem," said Lisa. "It's not every day we get to meet an Olympian god." And then she giggled. I could not believe what I was witnessing; Lisa was batting her eyes and actually flirting with Hermes. He, on the other hand, was slowly moving closer to where she stood. I had heard about relationships between gods and mortals, and I felt clearly at a disadvantage. After all, he was a god; I was merely an architect. So I figured I'd usher him out as subtly as possible.

"Well, Hermes, my good man," I said, "tell your father we're being treated very well. We appreciate your visit, you concern, and, not least of all, the opportunity to meet a fine Olympian. It's been a pleasure and let's hope our paths cross again. Goodnight and god-speed."

Hermes left without another word, and Lisa and I went back to bed.

"If you don't mind my saying, George, I think you were eager to get rid of our Olympian friend. You seemed jealous of that young man."

"Well, the way he was coming on to you, and with all I've read about gods and mortals, I figured he would have had you in bed right in front of me if I didn't do something about it."

"I'm flattered; I thought you were beyond jealousy.

"Jesus, Lisa, he's an Olympian! That's hardly fair competition. He probably has a few god-like moves I couldn't replicate in a million years."

"Why George, you make him sound more desirable than ever."

"Good night!" I said. "This has been one hell of a day, and it's time for it to end."

FOUR

We were up early the following morning, and within moments Polona and Thea appeared in our sitting room with a breakfast tray of bread, goat cheese, figs, and honey cakes. There was also a jug of wine, but it had been watered down to taste like grape juice. Zoe had mentioned earlier that drinking wine at full strength was considered barbaric. That may be, I thought, but drinking undiluted wine seemed to me a lot less barbaric than a toilet that was nothing more than hole in a stone slab. Another unsophisticated custom was the lack of utensils. I knew that forks did not become popular until after the Middle Ages, but aside from knives for slicing, one was expected to eat with his or her hands, a *modus operandi* most of us abandoned after infancy.

Polona and Thea were cheerful, as usual, and they asked if there was anything more they might provide. "Anything at all," they said. I looked at Lisa and smiled. She knew exactly what I was thinking. "A roll in the hay, George? Is that what you have in mind?"

"It was only a fantasy, my dear, but a tempting one, I admit."

Thea asked, "What is a roll in the hay?"

"Nothing much," I answered. "It's an activity occasionally enjoyed at home. But lately, not very often." Lisa responded to that comment with a raised eyebrow.

"Perhaps you can tell us more about it, and we can try to do it here," said Thea.

"I think we should forget it," said Lisa. "It would create too many complications."

We discussed earlier the means by which we might leave ancient Greece and return to the twenty-first century, but since we had no idea how we got here, we had even less of an idea how to return home. By the light of day some of the urgency we felt yesterday had dissipated. So, we decided that—for the moment—we would become tourists, which was the intent of our trip in the first place. After breakfast we headed for the Acropolis.

The stunning development of the Acropolis resulted from the inspiration, spirit, and power of Pericles, a leader who believed the glory of Athens should be revealed in visible form. Some years earlier, during the Persian Wars, this rocky outcrop high above the city was completely devastated, including the old Temple of Athena. Thus, Pericles began with a clean slate, employing the greatest talent in Athens and using only the finest materials available. He set out to produce a masterpiece that would make a statement to the world about the superiority of Athenian values, and in that goal he succeeded brilliantly.

Within a half-hour we reached the Propylaea, gateway to the holy structures of the Acropolis. Like most of the surrounding buildings it was composed of fine grain marble from nearby Mount Pentelicus. Adjacent to the Propylaea was the exquisite Ionic temple of Nike, dedicated to Wingless Victory, and beyond that were the Parthenon and the Erechtheion.

The Parthenon was perhaps the most famous architectural symbol ever conceived. It was one of the largest Greek temples ever built, and its sole purpose was to serve Athena, the virgin patroness of Athens. It was difficult to imagine how any structure could be so perfectly designed and flawlessly constructed. Stone joints, using no mortar, were tightly fitted and nearly invisible. And the sculptures, created by Phidias, attained the absolute pinnacle of artistic perfection.

Within the sanctuary of the Parthenon was Phidias' monumental statue of Athena. The figure was forty feet high, with ivory used for her flesh and gold for her draped clothing. Persians destroyed the statue around 600 A.D., so incredibly, we were the only modern people in history to view this remarkable work of art.

"Do you realize what we are seeing?" I asked Lisa. "No one has viewed this statue for more than fifteen hundred years. Doesn't that just blow your mind?"

"My mind was blown the moment Doros and his donkey cart appeared. This is all very nice, but, compared with suddenly finding myself in ancient Greece, this scores considerably lower on my mind-blowing scale.

Millions of people had visited the Parthenon during the past twenty-five hundred years, and most believed it to be the experience of a lifetime. Daphne du Maurier, the famous British author, said, *"As I looked on the Parthenon for the first time in my life, I found myself crying."* That is testament to the power of great art. It happened to me in Florence years earlier when viewing Michelangelo's David. Viewing the Parthenon, complete in all its perfection, had just become another emotional moment in my life. I, too, shed a few tears.

Before leaving the Acropolis we visited the nearby Erechtheion, perhaps the most unusual temple in all of Greece. The structure was uncharacteristically asymmetrical, built on two levels, and with one of the most famous porches in the world. The Porch of the Maidens had finely sculpted female forms used as columns to support its roof. It was breathtaking in its concept.

Suddenly, Lisa asked "Do you realize we've been on the Acropolis for nearly four hours?"

I glanced at my watch. "No, I wasn't aware of that. Are you getting bored?"

"Bored and hungry," she answered.

"Hold that thought," I said. "I just had an incredible idea. Since the Parthenon was completed only a couple of years ago, Ictinus, the architect, must still be alive. What if we could meet him? Wouldn't that be a monumental experience? It would be like meeting Michelangelo or Leonardo da Vinci. I'll bet Zoe could help us find him. Let's go back to the inn."

"Okay, I'll consider that," said Lisa, "*after* we get something to eat."

"I'm talking about one of the most extraordinary experiences of a lifetime, and you're concerned about your stomach? Where are your priorities?"

"Right now my first priority is getting fed; Ictinus can wait."

We returned to our inn, had some lunch, and then I spoke to Zoe.

"I'd like to ask an important favor. Is there anyone you know who might introduce us to the architect, Ictinus?"

She thought for a moment and replied, "I do have a friend who knows him, but I hear he is quite busy and may not have time to visit."

"Perhaps your friend could tell him that I am an architect who greatly admires his work. I have traveled a long distance to meet him and would consider this an enormous honor."

"I shall be happy to convey that message."

The very next morning Zoe came to tell me that Ictinus would be pleased to see us that day. I could not believe our luck. I was so excited by the news I hugged Zoe and kissed her squarely on the lips. She seemed a bit flustered, but finally smiled and said, "You are most welcome."

Ictinus's studio was located just behind the South Stoa, the portico on the south side of the Agora. We entered a small courtyard that was shaded by a single, mature olive tree. It was like walking on hallowed ground. We were about to meet one of the earliest giants of architectural history, and the significance of the moment made me tense. I rang a bell at the entrance and a teen-age boy opened the wooden door.

"May I help you," he asked.

"We are here to see Ictinus," I responded. "He is expecting us." Then I wondered if I should have said, *Mister* Ictinus? But since ancient Greeks had only a single name, that didn't sound right.

A few moments later the genius architect appeared. He was not at all what I expected. First of all, he looked young, perhaps in his mid-thirties or so. He was also movie star handsome, clean-shaven, and with flowing dark hair. His short tunic revealed the well-developed physique of an Olympian athlete.

"Welcome," he said warmly. "You must be the architect, George."

"Yes, and this is my wife Lisa. She is also a designer."

"I'm delighted to meet you," she said. And then she gave him a flirtatious smile.

"The pleasure is mine," said the charming architect. "I understand you come from a long distance. Where exactly is your home?"

"This will sound odd," I said, "but our country is one you have never heard of. It is a country that lies well beyond your Western Sea. It is called the United States."

"You're right, I have not heard of such a country. Did you take a boat to get here?"

"No, actually we flew here."

"You flew? Are you gods?"

"No, Ictinus, we are not gods, but our situation is difficult to explain. If I described the place we live and our way of life you would not understand it, and it would sound unbelievable. But we would rather speak to you about another subject—your marvelous architectural accomplishments. Your Parthenon is, without doubt, one of the finest structures ever built. You may not realize it, but thousands of years from today that structure will stand as one of the greatest architectural wonders of the world."

"That is very flattering, but, except for its size, I don't believe it differs that much from other similar projects. We believe that anything worth doing is worth doing to the best of our ability. We also believe that anything we create must have nobility and dignity worthy of our gods."

"Tell me," Ictinus, "why has your architecture never included the arch or vault? You might have produced spaces with greater spans and fewer columns."

"We know about arches, vaults, and domes," he answered, "but structural diversity, as well as originality for the sake of being original, has never interested us. We prefer the dependable post and beam system that has been used since the beginning of time. We avoid innovation, as we wish to perfect what we already know." I wondered what my creative colleagues back home would think of that antiquated notion.

"I understand that both you and Callicrates are credited as architects of the Parthenon. What part did he play in that project?"

"That remains a contentious matter. The position of Callicrates was Master of Works, which was a responsibility he carried out with great skill. But though he managed the construction for fifteen years, he was in no way accountable for the design. Now, however, he wishes to take architectural credit where no such credit is due. You know, Callicrates designed the Temple of Nike on the Acropolis, but you don't see me trying to take credit for that. What an egotistical ass that man has become! Honest to Zeus, the very thought of him exasperates me."

Ictinus paused, lowered his voice, and slowly regained his composure. "Now tell me about your work. Have you designed any temples?"

"Temple design is not common where we live. Some years ago, during what we call the neoclassical period, architects freely copied many Greek designs, but those structures were primarily banks or schools or government buildings. It is not the same today."

Lisa said, "You have a lovely studio. Would it be possible to see where you work?"

"Of course; let me show you my workspace and my home."

He led us to a large open space that had a high ceiling with exposed wood beams. The space contained several worktables at which assistants were building wooden scale models, while others carved full-size moldings and other details. At each worktable Ictinus stopped to explain what part of each project was being developed.

"Do you ever make drawings of your designs?" I asked.

"We do not draw, because workmen would be unable to decipher the intent of our design. We create models of wood and spend time at the site directing workers. Is that also your method?"

"No, we draw everything before we begin construction. Most drawings are now created on computers, but that is a device I could not begin to describe, nor would you believe it if I did."

Ictinus next led us to the small, sparsely furnished living area of his studio. "We have a small sitting area," he began, "a sleeping area for me and my companion, and a place to prepare food." It appeared as neatly designed as the finest modern apartment I had ever seen."

"Is your companion your wife?" asked Lisa.

"No, I am not married. My companion is the young boy who answered the door when you arrived. I am his mentor, and we have been together for two years. I educate him, protect him, and serve as his role model. I love him, however, as much as one might love a wife."

I had read about this aspect of ancient Greek life; it was common, and entirely accepted by this ancient society. In fact, there was no Greek word for homosexual; it was simply a part of love.

"Before you go," said Ictinus, "tell me, what is that odd bracelet on your wrist?"

"That is a wrist watch; it tells the time of day. It also glows, so you can read it at night."

"Is it as accurate as our sundials?"

"More accurate, and it works whether the sun is out or not. Also, it runs for a very long time without stopping. I notice we've been here for nearly an hour. I know you are busy, so we will leave now. We greatly appreciate your hospitality. This will remain one of the most extraordinary experiences of my life."

On our way back to the inn I said, "You seemed taken with Ictinus. Are you disappointed that he seems to prefer young men?"

"I bet I could turn him around in few minutes," she answered.

"What confidence! But I doubt that you'll have the opportunity."

When we returned to our inn I decided to see Zoe and discuss with her a matter that had troubled me since our arrival.

"I'm a bit confused," I began. "When we arrived you said you had been expecting us. That was the same thing Doros said when we met him. How could the two of you possibly know we even existed? And how did you know we would be staying here? Could you possibly clear up this mystery?"

"I do not know everything about this situation," she answered, "so I prefer to let someone else explain your presence here."

"Who did you have in mind?"

"If you can wait until tomorrow, that person will be here to see you."

"Can you tell me his name?"

"*Her* name is Aphrodite."

"Aphrodite, the goddess? What has she to do with this?"

"She will explain everything tomorrow. Please do not ask any further questions."

Later that night Lisa became surprisingly hostile. "Why did you have to start all that? Now some ancient goddess is involved, and who knows what new trouble that means? Why couldn't you just be quiet and leave things as they were?"

"Don't you understand? I'm trying to get us home, and if it takes a goddess, so be it."

I expected that tomorrow would bring a few answers. I only hoped they were answers that would lead us back to the twenty-first century.

FIVE

I tried to recall what I knew about Aphrodite—very little, as it turned out. But if we were to meet tomorrow to discuss our situation I felt obliged to learn the basic facts. I knew she was the goddess of love, beauty and sexuality, the Greek counterpart of the Roman goddess Venus. That was provocation enough to take out my copy of *Bullfinch's Mythology*, which I astutely packed before leaving home. I now reviewed those classic stories and learned some of what follows.

Aphrodite was not born in the conventional sense; her adult figure emerged from white sea foam, perfectly formed, eternally young, and stunningly beautiful. The foam arose when Uranus's son, Cronus, castrated his father and threw his testicles into the sea. Ouch! How bizarre was that? Because of Aphrodite's beauty, other gods feared that jealousy would disrupt the harmony among gods, so Zeus, the king of all gods, married her off to his son, Hephaestus, the only god who was born crippled and physically ugly. Hephaestus was the god of fire and forge who created thunderbolts for Zeus, arrows for Eros, and weapons and armor for other gods. He was actually a kind and peace-loving god, and in no way did he deserve the gift of an unfaithful wife.

As goddess of sexuality Aphrodite took her job seriously; she had a multitude of lovers, among whom were Ares, god of war and Adonis, god of beauty and desire. In fact, she apparently had a fling whenever she was in the mood, and according to legend, she was *always* in the mood. Aphrodite enchanted all she met and incited feeling of love and lust in all who gazed upon her beauty. I was beginning to think tomorrow's meeting might be a momentous experience, but I thought it best not to discuss any of that with Lisa.

In several legends Aphrodite was portrayed as vain, ill-tempered, and with a propensity to meddle in the affairs of mortals, often for her own amusement. Perhaps, I thought, this was a clue to tomorrow's meeting. Could she be meddling in *our* lives? As I read on, I discovered that Aphrodite was instrumental in causing the famous Trojan War, and what a story that was!

All the gods and goddesses, except for Eris, the goddess of strife and discord, were invited to an Olympian wedding. Eris, however, crashed the party with a golden apple that was inscribed with the words, *"To the Fairest"*. She threw the apple among the goddesses and then quickly left. Aphrodite, Hera, and Athena claimed to be the fairest and deserving of the apple. They placed the matter before Zeus, who put the choice in the hands of Paris, the mortal prince of Troy.

Each goddess attempted to bribe Paris. Hera offered him power, Athena offered wisdom, and Aphrodite offered marriage to Helen—the most beautiful mortal on earth. One can only guess what motivated Paris, but oddly, he chose the beauty of Helen over power and wisdom. Thus, Aphrodite won the beauty contest. Still, one troubling detail remained; Helen was already married to the King of Sparta. Aphrodite sent Paris to Sparta, where she made sure he was inflamed with lust for Helen. The two lovers fled Sparta and returned to Troy to be married.

Not quite the end of the story. Grecian troops sailed to Troy to avenge the abduction of Helen, and so began the ten-year Trojan War. The unintended consequence of Aphrodite's intervention led to the destruction and total annihilation of Troy. Suddenly, a feeling of dread overcame me; the same manipulative person who caused that epic drama was arriving tomorrow to explain the mystery of our presence in ancient Greece. I felt like crawling under the bed.

I slept little that night and awoke irritable and grouchy. To make matters worse, the weather was cool and overcast—our first day without brilliant sunshine. I took that as an ill omen.

"What's wrong with you today, Mr. Sunshine?" asked my sensitive wife.

"Have you forgotten? An important person—a genuine goddess, in fact—will soon arrive to reveal the mystery of our sudden appearance in ancient Greece? Does that ring a bell?"

"Oh that. Not to worry, I can hold my own with any old Greek floozy."

"For your information, this was the floozy who just happened to start the Trojan War. What's more, she has mythical powers and the entire Olympian family of gods to back her up."

"You worry too much, George."

Perhaps she was right; I did worry too much. Perhaps there was nothing to worry about. Perhaps Aphrodite would arrive with a pair of one-way, first class tickets from ancient Athens to Los Angeles, a destination that wouldn't even exist for another two thousand years. Sure, what were the odds of that? Or just maybe Aphrodite was coming here to have a few laughs at our expense.

We were sitting in our courtyard late that morning when Zoe appeared to announce a guest was here to see us. "Is it you-know-who?" I asked.

"I am pleased to say that we welcome the honorable goddess of love, beauty, pleasure, and procreation—Aphrodite." All that was missing was a triumphant blare of trumpets. The figure that appeared wore a dark, full-length cloak with a hood that covered much of her face.

"I assume," she said, "you are George and Lisa." Her voice was like a mellow instrument.

"You assume right," I answered, "but I suppose you already knew that, what with your goddess-like powers and such."

"Stop that," whispered Lisa, "this is no time for sarcasm."

"I know much about you," said Aphrodite, "but I had only a vague idea of your appearance."

"Let me get right to the point," I said. "Have you any idea how we got here, and how we might return home. Is there anything you can tell us about that?"

"You may want to remain with us a bit longer before you decide that going home is what you really want. But first, let me tell you *why* you are here. As you know, I am the goddess of love, and my responsibility is to promote love where none exists, encourage love when it malfunctions, and restore love after it is badly damaged. I'm afraid your relationship falls into every one of those unfortunate categories. You two are perfect examples of those who require my help and counsel. In addition, I believe your relationship, unlike most others, is truly worth saving."

"You mean," said Lisa, "all this has something to do with our rotten marriage? If you looked around you'd find plenty of people with worse marriages than ours, and you don't see any of them being shipped off to some ancient civilization. Out of the millions of unhappy marriages in this world why on earth would you choose us? How did you even *know* about us? Are there Greek spies in Los Angeles with nothing better to do than stalk people in lousy relationships?"

"Greek gods have incredible powers that are difficult for mere mortals to understand. We know about everything and everyone— everywhere. Yours, however, is a special case. You two happen to reflect, to a remarkable degree, the philosophy of our extraordinary civilization. You are creative and strong-willed people who believe in freedom, honor, and respect for the individual. You also recognize that physical well-being is equally as important as mental well-being. You are fine examples of those who strive for physical perfection. In other words, you represent all that excites and exalts those who would aspire to be part of this great and noble Hellenic society."

"Well, thank you," said Lisa. "That sounded like a genuine compliment. You know I work out with a personal trainer every other day, and George here plays tennis twice a week."

"That's enough, Lisa." I said. "We're not applying to join a country club, you know."

"Don't tell me what to say. I think it's important that Aphrodite knows we take physical fitness seriously. At least I do."

"Getting back to the question," I said to Aphrodite, "can you help us return home?"

"Of course, if that is really what you want. After all, I brought you here, didn't I?"

"Well, what do we have to do to leave?" I asked. "Can we kiss and make up, or perhaps sign an agreement never to quarrel again? Would that do it?"

"I fear you are not taking this seriously, George. Your loving relationship is damaged and defective; it needs to be repaired. I assure you, this is a crucial matter. It is also more complicated than you think. You know, if I wanted, I could have my companion, Eros, shoot you with one of his arrows, and you would be crazy in love and locked in each other's arms within minutes. But that might not endure for the longer term."

"So, what have you in mind?" I asked.

"We will discuss that in good time." More mystery. Would we ever get a straight answer from an ancient Greek?

"We have heard of your exceptional beauty, Aphrodite. Would you be kind enough to remove your hood so we can view a bit more of your face."

"Of course, but let us go into your sitting room."

We left the courtyard and settled in the sitting room, at which point Aphrodite untied the bow of her hood. It fell away from her face revealing the most exquisite features and flawless complexion I had ever seen. Her lustrous hair cascaded over her shoulders, her eyes were deeper than the green of the sea, and her lips were moist and luscious, as if begging to be kissed. In the next moment her robe fell to the floor, and even Lisa gasped at the sight before us. Aphrodite was completely nude. Completely! Her shoulders, breasts, waist, hips, and legs were more perfectly formed and sensually arranged than one could possibly imagine. She was absolutely dazzling and even more ideal than the finest statue by Phidias, the greatest Greek sculptor who ever lived.

"I can see that no description I've read does justice to your beauty," I said. "I certainly understand why you drive men wild with desire. You are truly magnificent!"

"Well, of course, George. Good heavens, I *am* a goddess, you know."

"And not a particularly modest one," said Lisa.

"No need for sarcasm," said Aphrodite sharply. "This is not a competition. If it were, you wouldn't stand a chance, I assure you. I would possess your George faster than the blink of an eye. So don't tempt me."

"I happen to know George better than you," said Lisa, "and I think you're wrong."

At that point Aphrodite walked over to me, reached for my right hand, and placed it on her bare breast. She held it there for a few moments and then asked, "How does that feel, George?"

I was dizzy with desire but knew this was a predicament with no good answer. Admitting my lust for Aphrodite would wound Lisa, and if Aphrodite believed I was totally unaffected by her bold move, she might very well turn me into a horned toad. So I remained silent.

"You need not say a word," she said. "I can see by the folds in your tunic it is having the desired affect. You see, Lisa, a goddess of pleasure knows well her subject."

"Nonsense," said Lisa. "I could have the very same affect on him."

"But you have not done so for months. Ability and desire must go hand in hand. It is possible you once had the ability, but desire has been absent for a long time."

At that moment there was a knock on the door and in walked a handsome and well-built young man wearing a scant piece of fabric that served as a loincloth.

"What are you doing here?" asked the startled Aphrodite.

"Looking for you. What is that man doing with his hand on your breast?" I immediately pulled my hand away, yet it continued to tingle for several moments. I sensed something hostile and frightening about this stranger, and it made me uncomfortable.

"That is none of your concern. I have brought this couple here for my own purpose."

"Who is this guy?" I asked.

"A friend," she answered.

"A friend? I am no mere friend; I am Aphrodite's lover. My name is Ares."

"Ares, the god of war?

"Yes; I assume you have heard of me."

Indeed I had. Ares, the god of war, resided on Mount Olympus, where he was generally disliked and feared by other gods. He was known for his cruelty and bloodlust, but admired for being a fearless warrior. Ares had no spouse; and though his first love was bloody conflict, a close second was his love for Aphrodite, with whom he carried on a lengthy adulterous affair.

What she saw in him remained a mystery. Historians have guessed she was attracted by his ruthless and callous behavior, the way good girls are often fascinated by bad boys. If opposites attract, no more appropriate match could be imagined than the god of war and the goddess of love. Years ago there was a popular aphorism: *Make love, not war*. Apparently Aphrodite and Ares did a great deal of both.

"I have heard of you, Ares. When it comes to making war you apparently have no equal."

"Yes, I am quite proud of that."

"I would think one would be prouder of making peace; that would be constructive. As an architect I believe building is more honorable than destroying."

"Who is this arrogant mortal?" Ares asked of Aphrodite.

"He is someone in whom I have an interest," she replied.

"Well I think he is a fool, and I don't like him."

"My wife often thinks the same," I said. "You two may have something in common."

"That's not entirely true," said Lisa. She seemed embarrassed by the thought.

"Well if it's not true, then what are we doing here discussing our rotten marriage with a couple of Greek gods? Do you realize how insane this is? Our relationship is on life support and at any minute I figure someone's going to pull the plug. Honest to God—and I don't mean these two—I'm ready to give it up. Let's get the hell out of here and forget this bad dream ever happened."

"But you haven't allowed me to help you," said Aphrodite. "You have no idea what I am capable of doing for you. You must not give up so soon."

"Let him go," said Ares. "He's a bigger fool than I thought, and I still don't like him."

"Stay out of this," said Lisa. "This is none of your business, you hostile jackass."

"You cannot speak to me that way. I am an Olympian god!"

"You are also an Olympian asshole!" shouted Lisa.

"Please," said Aphrodite, "let us be civilized. Ares, you must leave now. George and Lisa, kindly be seated. We shall make a plan for your future."

Ares left without a goodbye, and Aphrodite took her seat, still as appealingly nude as ever.

"Before we continue," said Lisa, "would you mind putting on your cloak? George may have trouble concentrating on what you have to say."

"I'm capable of doing more than one thing at a time," I said.

Nevertheless, Aphrodite covered up and said, "I have decided that our next step will be a trip to Delphi. We shall consult the Oracle about you two, and proceed from there. I will make the arrangements and we shall leave in the morning."

"Delphi?" I said. "Well, why not? We planned to visit there anyway." I figured it wouldn't be a total loss, but who could possibly guess what we were about to learn.

SIX

Delphi was situated on the slopes of Mount Parnassus, about a hundred miles northwest of Athens. It occurred to me that if we traveled there in Doros' donkey cart it would take at least twelve hours, most likely twelve genuinely uncomfortable hours. Little did I know that Aphrodite had other plans. She arrived early that morning, and as we left the inn I noticed a large white horse standing near the entrance. And then I almost sprained my neck as I did a swift double take. The horse had wings! Honest to God, huge wings sprouted from his sides, each at least eight feet long. "I can't believe it," said Lisa. "This is so incredibly mythological!"

"This," said Aphrodite, "is Pegasus. He will get us to Delphi in a few minutes."

A few minutes? Who needed supersonic travel? We had Pegasus! I recently read the myth about Pegasus and found it typically bizarre. His mother was Medusa, a beautiful maiden who was caretaker at Athena's temple. Poseidon, god of the sea, fell in love with Medusa and seduced her inside the temple. This so enraged Athena, she punished— not Poseidon the seducer—but innocent Medusa, the victim of the seduction. She transformed her into a horrible monster with gruesome face and serpents for hair. Years later Medusa was killed by Perseus, a son of Zeus, and from the blood of her severed head sprang Pegasus.

Once again I wondered—who makes up this stuff? Nothing in Greek mythology was simple or predictable, and invariably it involved sex and violence. In any event, Pegasus was loved and admired by all the gods, and he was known to travel faster than the wind.

"Climb on," ordered Aphrodite, "we're off to Delphi."

The three of us mounted Pegasus, whose back was large enough to carry us comfortably. Lisa sat near the horse's neck clutching his mane, I was behind her, and Aphrodite brought up the rear. She threw her arms around my waist, kicked the flanks of our equine transport, and we swiftly arose. What an incredible sensation! In a moment we were above Athens and viewing the entire city, as one would see it from a low-flying plane. Strangely, I felt little fear, even though there was no saddle, no seat belt, or anything but Lisa's waist to hold onto.

"How are you doing?" I asked Lisa.

"I'm scared to death, but this is the greatest thrill I've ever had."

"Those were your exact words the night we first made love."

"Okay, second greatest thrill."

We were traveling at blazing speed over the rocky terrain below, and occasionally a farmer or shepherd would look up and wave to us. I would have waved back, but I feared losing my grip and falling to my death. Meanwhile, Lisa was giggling out of pure joy, and even Aphrodite was humming a pleasant tune that sounded, oddly, like that old Sinatra classic, *Fly Me To The Moon*. Who knew that riding an ancient, mythological beast could bring such pure, unadulterated delight?

In no time we arrived at Delphi. As we circled the city I recognized some of the familiar temples and monuments. Pegasus aimed for an open field and set down as lightly as a leaf falling from a tree. I was mightily impressed and thought how wonderful it would be to have such a practical pet of my own. I could see myself flying over Los

Angeles freeways and feeling superior to those below stuck in rush-hour traffic. They would be cursing my winged horse sailing above them, and I would wave condescendingly, like someone literally on his high horse. What a splendid fantasy! Of course there would be a downside; I'd have to feed the beast and shovel horseshit every day; but I figured it would be well worth it.

We headed for the Delphic Oracle to learn what we could from this prestigious source of wisdom. The priestess who made the wise pronouncements was called the Pythia. Originally this was a young virgin, because great emphasis was put on the Oracle's chastity and purity. However, years earlier a horny young supplicant became enamored with the Pythia's beauty, carried her away and, as they say, "relieved her of her virginity". It was then decreed that Pythias would be chosen from among women who were at least fifty years of age.

The Pythia sat on a tripod built over a chasm that emitted brain-altering vapors. As the Pythia began to babble, a priest in attendance would interpret the generally incoherent message. Interpretations were usually logical, but often as cryptic and ambiguous as astrological forecasts. For example: *Step aside now at your own risk.* Or, *Pursue your original assumption.* Or one of my favorites, *Run now, and run fast.*

There was an interesting story about Croesus, the last king of Lydia that served to caution those who claimed to understand the Oracle's intent. Croesus wanted to determine if it was wise to invade a neighboring country. He received the following answer: *Going to war will cause destruction of a great empire.* He went to war, was soundly defeated, and the great empire destroyed was his very own.

How anyone could find an oracle helpful was a mystery, and I realized it was mostly my problem. To begin with, I was not very spiritual. I invariably doubted notions that could not be proved, and I remained skeptical of all sacred pronouncements. Nevertheless, here we were, and Aphrodite was convinced this would be a useful exercise. And if not, at least we had one hell of a ride on a flying horse.

Dealing with the Oracle was rigidly structured in several prescribed steps. The first of these was the journey to Delphi, during which the Oracle's ability to provide answers would strongly motivate the supplicant to formulate his or her thoughts concisely. I felt we were already behind your average supplicant on that one.

Next was the preparation of the supplicant, including an interview by the priest in attendance. The priest reviewed rules of conduct before the Oracle and how the questions were to be framed. Questions to the Oracle were meant to elicit advice that would shape future action. Based on earlier conversations Aphrodite had prepared three questions—the maximum allowed—and I found it difficult to argue with her wording:

- How do we fall in love again?
- Will our marriage survive?
- How can we become parents?

Lisa and I agreed that those were the most important problems that shaped our contentious relationship. In fact, during earlier discussions we were—much to my surprise—in remarkable agreement.

The next step was visiting the Oracle, putting our questions to the Pythia, and departing immediately after receiving the answers.

"Nervous?" I asked.

"A little," she said. "I'm afraid of what I might hear."

"Just remember this: we're in ancient Greece; the Oracle has never advised an American from the twenty-first century. So maybe none of this will make sense. And regardless of what she says, we're going to be okay. I just know it."

"Well, thanks for saying that."

Aphrodite led us to the temple entrance and then departed. As we entered the large shrine the attending priest met us and silently guided us to the sanctuary. The Pythia was sitting at the center of this space on her three-legged stool, and beneath the stool were visible vapors rising from the fissure below. The Pythia was dressed in an unadorned, full-length, white robe and was barefoot. Her skin was deathly pale and her tangled hair looked like a chaotic pile of recently mowed hay. Her head rolled uncontrollably as incoherent sounds emanated from the depths of her throat. She appeared to be in such a deep trance I wondered whether she even knew she had visitors. I watched the priest for some sign that the Pythia was ready for our questions, but he stood silently with his eyes closed.

I began to wonder what I was doing there. The Pythia looked totally stoned and ready to pass out, and I could swear the priest was napping and about to keel over. What a pair! It felt like I was in some ancient psychiatric ward. How could anything useful come from this?

Just then the old lady uttered a shriek that almost stopped my heart. "What the hell?" I said. "What's happening?"

"The Pythia is ready for your questions," said the drowsy priest.

I cleared my throat. "Tell me, oh wise Oracle, how do we fall in love again?"

The Pythia began to mumble, and her head rolled around so vigorously, I though it might actually fly off her neck.

The priest strained to hear what sounded like garbled sound effects coming out of her mouth. Then he said, "You must return to the place where you first loved."

"What on earth does that mean? asked Lisa. "First loved who? Or what?

"Your next question," prompted the priest.

"Will our marriage survive?" I asked.

Again the Pythia went through her odd contortions as she mumbled an answer. The priest closed his eyes and was quiet for such a long time

I feared he might have dozed off again. Then he said, "All will remain the same, but there will be changes."

"That makes no sense," I said. "How can it remain the same if there are changes?"

Finally we came to the last question, the one most important to Lisa.

"How can we become parents?"

The Pythia was quiet for a moment, and then she became more agitated than ever. I thought for a moment she would leap off her stool and attack the insolent fools who dared to waste her time with such nonsense. Her expression said, "What a dumb-ass question!" The priest listened to her mumbles intently and then said, "It will happen through love."

"Are you sure that's what she said?" asked Lisa. "Doesn't she know we've made love about a million times? Is that some kind of Pythian joke?"

"The Oracle knows everything," said the priest, "and that is her answer to your question."

As there was nothing more to say, we thanked the priest, nodded at the Pythia, who appeared loopier than ever, and left.

Aphrodite greeted us outside the temple and asked what we had learned from the Oracle.

"That's difficult to know," I said. "We're really confused. The answers to our questions could have different interpretations, and I suppose they depend on how we feel about our marriage and each other. We really have to think about this."

We headed for the Temple of Apollo, but our hearts were not into sightseeing. There were those mysterious pronouncements to consider. So I asked Aphrodite if we could return to Athens to talk things over. "Of course," she said.

During our visit to the Oracle, Pegasus had been happily grazing in a nearby field. He must have been happy because when he saw us he reared up on his hind legs and gave a heartfelt whinny. We climbed aboard our mythological steed and flew south toward Athens. The return trip was equally as thrilling as the earlier one, and within minutes we were back at our inn.

"I must leave you now," said Aphrodite, "but there is much more we will discuss tomorrow. Meanwhile, remain vigilant. My friend Ares has taken a dislike to you, and he has the power to cause much trouble." In addition to our other problems, it now appeared we had made an Olympian enemy. We needed that like a not-so-mythical hole in the head.

"When we reached our room Lisa began her attack. "So, Mr. Moral Authority, you had to tell Ares he had it all wrong. It's more honorable to build than destroy, you said. Don't you know he's the god of war, for Christ's sake? Do you know what gods of war do? They make war, that's what they do! What the hell were you thinking, George?"

"Now just a minute. If I remember correctly, it was you who called him an Olympian asshole. How could you possibly think that endearing term would be well received? If Ares is upset with us, it might be because of you and your foul mouth."

"Well, there's probably no point in arguing over Ares," she said. "Whatever happens is beyond out control anyway. If he decides to turn us into a couple of silly geese we might be able to fly home." Then she smiled. "Now I think we should talk about what we heard today in Delphi."

"I've been thinking about that," I said, "and I have an idea about the first question. How do we fall in love again, we asked, and she said, 'Return to the place where you first loved.' Do you remember our first job in San Francisco? We went to see our client, and we stayed at a small hotel near Fisherman's Wharf. That night you knocked on the door to my room and said you wanted to discuss the job. But instead we made love all night. It was the most thrilling night of my life. 'Return to the place where you first loved,' the Oracle said. It's *got* to be San Francisco!"

"Oh God, what memories!" said Lisa. "I do remember that night, and I always will."

"The second answer is more confusing. The Oracle said. 'All will remain the same, but there will be changes.' In other words, it appears our marriage *will* survive, but not in its current state. 'There will be changes,' the Oracle said."

"There would have to be," said Lisa. "Our marriage hasn't worked for years. But what kind of changes? And changes by you or me or something else we haven't even thought of?"

"I have no idea," I said.

"What about the last answer?" asked Lisa. "She said that becoming parents would happen through love. Did she really think we haven't tried to make a baby? She might as well have suggested we try prayer."

"Maybe she knows something we don't," I said. "But if those answers are supposed to guide our future, I can't imagine how that will happen. I feel like I did before; when it comes to us, I'm afraid we're pretty much on our own."

So there we were, just as before, on our own. And then I wondered: what do we do now?

SEVEN

The fear and danger I felt from Ares kept me up half the night. There was no doubt in my mind that he was the most dangerous god residing on Mount Olympus. With parents like Zeus and Hera, he should have had a model childhood, but Ares was unloved from the start, and neither parent had much sympathy for his activities. His father once said, "You are the most hateful of all gods," and Ares did his best to live up to that assessment.

The story of Ares' relationship with Adonis, the god of desire, was a clue to his aggression. When Aphrodite first gazed on the infant Adonis she was enchanted by his beauty. She entrusted him to Persephone, goddess of the underworld, to care for him until he grew up. As the years passed and Adonis grew into a handsome youth, Persephone also became enamored of Adonis and refused to give him up. Zeus settled the dispute between the two goddesses by permitting Adonis to live with each goddess for four months and then live alone for the final four months of each year.

To add a further complication, Persephone was also carrying on with Ares, our new enemy. At some point she mentioned to him, "Aphrodite has a new lover, and you have little chance with her because he is incredibly gorgeous." This, of course, enraged Ares, who then turned himself into a wild boar and killed Adonis in hunting "accident". Both goddesses were so devastated by the loss of their lover that Zeus eventually declared, "Adonis is not really dead!" So the resurrected god of desire ended up spending six months of each year with Aphrodite *and* Persephone.

By this time it was clear that nearly every ancient god, goddess, and mortal was at one time or another sleeping with every other god, goddess, and mortal. In addition, I realized that Ares was a vicious killer who would use every trick in the book to make our life miserable. Other than avoiding him, I had no idea how we could protect ourselves from this mythological psychopath.

Meanwhile, in her continuing effort to repair our ailing marriage Aphrodite arranged for us to meet with a person she characterized as the wisest person in Athens. "My brilliant friend," she said, "may have the answers you seek." If he was that bright, I thought, perhaps he could suggest a way to deal with Ares. Of course saving our marriage was paramount, but living long enough to enjoy our newfound love was pretty high on the list as well.

We followed the instructions given us and arrived at a modest house located a few blocks from the Agora. I knocked on the door and waited. There was no response, so I knocked again—this time more loudly. Finally the door opened. I was suddenly transfixed and totally speechless. Oh no, I thought, this can't possibly be him—could it? But there he stood, as profoundly unattractive as historians through the ages had described him.

There was the squat figure, the large belly, flat face with wide-set bulging eyes, upturned nose with flaring nostrils, and scant hair that appeared as unkempt as his scraggly beard. I had no doubt that standing before us was Socrates! This was not Socrates Papadopoulos, who ran the hardware store in Santa Monica, nor was it Socrates Mendelssohn, who sliced pastrami at our local delicatessen. This was the original, the one and only Socrates, the greatest Athenian philosopher who ever lived—and apparently still did!

"How can I help you?" he asked.

The voice of this noble man was clear and melodious, and his eyes sparkled. I recalled Lord Byron's description: *"Socrates, the earth's perfection of mental beauty and personification of all virtue who was the inspiration in every age for how one should live one's life".*

"My name is George," I said, "and this is my wife, Lisa."

"You'll have to speak up, young man. My hearing isn't what it used to be."

I repeated my introduction a bit louder, to which he replied, "Strange names."

"Yes, well, let me tell you why we are here. We've had some marital difficulties," I began, "and our friend, Aphrodite, suggested that we discuss them with you."

"Please come in and have a seat; we shall consider your problem. Let me get some wine." The house was relatively austere and simply furnished. Several pieces of finely painted pottery provided the only decoration. When we were comfortably seated, Socrates began to speak in a soft voice. "So, how is my old friend, Aphrodite? We have not seen one another for a long time."

"She is well and sends kindest regards."

"Kindest regards? She sends regards, but not love? How things do change."

"Was love involved?" asked Lisa.

"Oh yes, we had our little dalliance, and it was memorable. She is the goddess of love and beauty, you know, and no other I've known is quite as enchanting. She glories in her nakedness, her sexuality is free from ambivalence, and she exemplifies the wonder and power of femininity. She is an inspired lover, a divine goddess, and the very essence of sexual pleasure."

"It sounds as though you still have strong feelings for her," said Lisa.

"She is eternally young, and I am old. She is a goddess, and I am mortal. There is much that keeps us apart, but memories are unmindful of such details, and it is my memories that will forever connect us."

"There was a situation where we come from that was quite similar to yours," I said. "One of the world's most brilliant scientists, who was in the twilight of his career, developed a connection with a young woman of great beauty. His name was Albert Einstein, and she was an actress named Marilyn Monroe. They were both rather famous, and people could not understand the relationship. But I suspect you could readily empathize with their circumstances."

"I have not heard of these people," said Socrates, "but I do understand how beauty of the intellect can arouse a desire equal to that of physical beauty. Now let us speak about the problem that brought you here. Human relationships are often complicated. I have always believed, whether marriage or celibacy, let a man take which course he will, and he will be sure to repent." And then he giggled. "That was a joke," he added.

"Very amusing," I said, "but it's a bit late for that. We've been married for several years and are trying to avoid repentance. We hoped your wisdom would help us see where we may have gone wrong and what we might do to correct the situation."

"There is something else you should understand," said Socrates. "I am not an authority on anything, but I do know this: even the most loving marriages occasionally experience terrible times. Humans are imperfect and emotions are unpredictable. Quarrels may lead to discord, and discord is the enemy of true love."

"How is it, Socrates, that you are not married?" asked Lisa.

"Oh, but I *am* married. My wife of several years is Xanthippe, who is somewhat younger than I and quite independent. Some have described her as the most obstinate mortal that ever was or ever will be."

"Why would you choose such an unmanageable partner?" I asked.

"It is said that skilled horsemen avoid the most docile animals; they prefer high-spirited ones. The idea is that if one can control these, one will easily manage any other horse."

"But a wife is not a horse," I said, stating the obvious.

"No, but since I wish to deal with others, I have provided myself with this wife. If I can put up with her, I shall learn to get along with other human beings. Furthermore, demanding that Xanthippe become the perfect embodiment of my personal desires would not be as rewarding as developing my own character. Thus, I view our quarrels and tantrums as opportunities for me to learn and grow stronger. This way may not be for everyone, but it is the way I have chosen."

"That is certainly an original idea," said Lisa. "Most people I know believe spouses should try to compromise to make each other happy."

"Yes, but when that doesn't work out," said Socrates, "they may take a lover or simply leave the nest. I am not sure that is a better solution."

"But didn't you take Aphrodite as your lover?"

"True, but I am not a perfect human being. Besides, our society neither chastises nor condones such conduct. It is a matter left to the individual."

"So what is one to believe?"

"Marriage, I think, is something to be encouraged. If you get a good wife, you will become happy; if you get a bad one, you will become— like me—a philosopher." Then he giggled again. When the laughter stopped, Socrates' expression became serious. "There is one more thing," he said, "and this is quite important. Love finds a way. By that I mean, when love is true, one need not search for it; it will find you. It will change your heart, your life, and your very soul. That is the amazing power of true love."

When I considered Socrates' words, love seemed a simple matter. But was he right? If love finds a way, why were Lisa and I struggling like two cats in a bag? It had to be more complicated.

"Now let us discuss your situation," said Socrates. "An honest investigation should reveal knowledge of your true selves. Truth, I believe, is the highest virtue and the beginning of wisdom. And wisdom begins when one realizes he knows nothing."

Lisa whispered to me, "Now there's something for you to think about." I ignored the comment but was nonetheless annoyed.

"I assume you were once in love," said Socrates.

"Yes, we were," I answered.

"And now?"

"I still love her," I said, "but she has become more like your Xanthippe—a bit of a shrew."

"And Lisa," asked Socrates, "how do you feel about George?"

"I don't know. I once adored him and felt he was the only man on earth with whom I wanted to spend my life. I genuinely felt a deep love for him. But there have been so many quarrels, so much unhappiness, I cannot forget the terrible times we have experienced."

"Did the good times outweigh the bad times?" asked Socrates.

"That is not easy to measure. If one loves the good times but hates the bad times what is the answer to that question?"

Socrates sat quietly for a few moments considering that comment. Then he asked, "Do you think your life would be happier without George?"

Lisa did not answer at once. Her expression appeared pained as she considered the possibility of our being apart. "He makes me laugh," she said, "and I would miss that. He can also be warm and loving, but I have not seen that side of him for a long time."

"How about you, George? Would you be happier without Lisa?"

"I don't think so. We have fallen into some bad habits, and there are times when I wish I could just put her in a basket and drop her off on some distant doorstep. But there is much about her I truly love and would unquestionably miss."

"When was the last time you two shared a romantic moment?" asked Socrates.

"It's been a long time," I said. "I don't handle rejection well. As a result, I stopped making romantic advances long ago."

"I believed he no longer found me attractive," said Lisa. "I thought he must hate me."

"Oh no! You are so wrong," I said. "I simply thought our romance was over."

"So," said Socrates, "it appears you two have not communicated your true feelings. How very sad! We must do something about that."

"It's especially sad since we've spent so much time and money with therapists who never approached the source of our problem, as we have done today."

"There is one more problem of which we have not spoken," said Lisa. "George has a condition that precludes our ever having a child. It is a matter of great disappointment to me and the origin of much of my insecurity and unhappiness."

"Ah, children," said Socrates, "they are both the source of joy and despair. One should consider carefully whether or not having them is desirable. Children today have little respect for their elders; they have contempt for authority, and most lack proper manners. Why would anyone wish to be surrounded by such uncivilized mortals? I have three sons, and I can tell you that being a parent is not always a delight. My children rarely visit and they show little concern for their father."

"Why Socrates," said Lisa, "you sound very much like a Jewish mother."

In fact, his complaint hit just the right whiny note, but Lisa's comment appeared to sail right over his head. He paused for a moment and then continued his discourse. "Nevertheless, if parenting is what you desire there are remedies for nearly every condition."

"I have tried them all," I said, "and sadly, none has worked."

"Have you tried walnuts?"

"Walnuts? Is this another joke?"

"Not at all. Walnuts are reputed to be an effective aphrodisiac. Let me tell you about Dionysus, the god of fertility. He was madly in love with the goddess Caryae, and when she died he was absolutely devastated. He transformed her lifeless body into a walnut tree, and since that time walnuts have become a symbol of love and fertility. Walnuts are often served at weddings and frequently offered to guests as love tokens. I am surprised you have not heard of this."

I began to wonder why none of my twenty-first-century medical specialists had mentioned walnuts. I had the cynical feeling they preferred to profit from pharmaceuticals, or perhaps, like me, they believed the appropriate use of walnuts was atop a hot fudge sundae.

"There is more for us to discuss," said Socrates," but I have no more time today. Possibly you can return again and we can continue our inquiry. I think there is more to discuss."

"Just one more question before we leave," I said. "Ares, the god of war, has become an enemy, and we wonder if you have any suggestion how we might prevent a confrontation. He appears unbalanced and particularly dangerous."

"My advice is to avoid Ares. He is a treacherous enemy and quite unpredictable. If you meet him again you must flatter him; his ego is larger than the Great Sphinx of Egypt. Ares is not terribly bright, and he will not know your true feelings. So shower him with flattery, and you will survive."

"And if that doesn't work?" asked Lisa.

"Well then, you will have no further need of advice. You will be finished."

Given that choice our strategy was obvious; we would flatter Ares until the cows came home. We thanked Socrates, said good-bye, and walked out into the sunlight.

"What a fascinating visit!" said Lisa. "I can barely digest everything we spoke about. What do you think, George?"

"All I can think of is walnuts. Walnuts! Who would have guessed? I also think there's a glimmer of hope we may survive Ares. And as for us, well, if the old philosopher is right, love will find a way."

EIGHT

We strolled quietly down the street, lost in our thought about the time spent with Socrates. Suddenly, from behind us, we heard the sound of galloping hooves. I turned and was shocked to see two chariots racing down the street. A pair of charging horses pulled each chariot, and the drivers carried long spears. My thoughts turned to that exciting scene out of the old movie Ben-Hur—you know, that early Christian melodrama—and I thought a film crew must be in town making a sequel. Then the realization hit me: This is ancient Greece, you nitwit; movies won't be invented for another two thousand years.

Then my pulse accelerated as I noticed the chariots were heading right at us! "Holy shit!" I cried. I grabbed Lisa by the arm and we dashed across the street towards an open courtyard.

As they came nearer I could see the drivers' eyes glowing with hatred and their faces contorted into sinister scowls. What the hell is going on? Are we on someone's hit list? When they were almost upon us I picked up Lisa by the waist and sprinted into the courtyard. Almost simultaneously the drivers hurled their spears in our direction. They missed us by mere inches and landed harmlessly against the wall of the building.

"They're trying to kill us!" Lisa cried hysterically.

"You're right, but thank God they missed."

"Who are they?"

"I have no idea, but I'd be willing to bet they know Ares."

"Of course they know Ares," said an elderly man in the courtyard where we stood. "He is their father, and they are his twin sons, Deimos and Phobos."

"Who are you?" I asked.

"I am Aristophanes, and you are in the courtyard of my house."

The name sounded familiar, but I was sure we had not met. Aristophanes was a heavyset, middle-aged man with white, curly hair and bushy beard. In the appropriate outfit he might have made a splendid Santa Claus. He also wore what I now assumed was the standard male Greek outfit—a mid-thigh-length white tunic and leather sandals.

"Forgive our barging in like this," I said, "but it probably saved our lives. Did you say these are Ares' sons? What can you tell us about them?"

"They are as ruthless and bloodthirsty as their father. Deimos is the god of fear and dread, and Phobos is the god of terror and panic. It is said that Aphrodite is their mother, though few believe the goddess of love could be the mother of such horrifying gods."

That's all we needed, I thought. In addition to Ares we now had the whole damn family tree crashing down on us. Sadly, we never had the chance to appease Ares, and I wondered if Socrates had any idea how to deal with his relatives. I also wondered if we'd live long enough to find out.

"Do you think they'll be back," I asked.

"I doubt it," said Aristophanes. "I suspect they were merely trying to frighten you. They are excellent warriors and outstanding marksmen; if they wanted to kill you they probably would have succeeded. I think they were sending a message. If you are concerned about them returning, perhaps you should remain here a while." Aristophanes led us into his modest house and offered us some wine. As we sat there quietly sipping our drinks and waiting for our pulses to slow, our host asked, "What prompted Deimos and Phobos to attack you? You hardly appear threatening."

"We didn't even know those delinquents existed until ten minutes ago," I answered. "But we recently had some quarrelsome words with their father, and I think he is behind this attack. Our dispute with Ares was contentious, but it hardly warranted attempted murder. Do you suppose homicide is his solution to everything?"

"Yes, I think it is. Ares has never been known for subtlety. By the way, who are you two? Are you citizens of Athens?"

"My name is George and this is Lisa, my wife. We are visitors to your city, and until this afternoon, relatively pleased to be here. We come from a land very far from here, and if we survive Ares' vengeance we hope to return there one day."

"You say you are from a distant land, and though your names are quite foreign you speak our language without the trace of an accent. How do you account for that?"

"I wish I *could* account for that. Believe me, we are as mystified as you." Aristophanes gave me a quizzical look, but he did not pursue the subject.

Lisa had been sitting quietly, but her body was rigid, fists clenched, and she wore a grim expression. It was obvious that her outrage over the attack was intensifying, and she seemed ready to erupt. "Tell me, Aristophanes," she began, "is there an authority here that deals with attempted assassination? I mean, is it permissible for any Athenian degenerate to run wild in public and throw spears at people?"

"Certainly not; that sort of activity is not tolerated here or in any other civilized society. We have a system that deals with those who ignore the rules of decency. But, unfortunately, Deimos and Phobos are gods, and as such, it is their peers who must judge them."

"Like who?" asked Lisa. "Zeus himself, or any old god on your weird totem pole?"

"I realize you are upset, Lisa, but sarcasm is unnecessary. For your information, Themis is the goddess of justice. She determines the divine order of all activities. Themis shares her temple with Nemesis, who is the god of retribution. When Themis determines that a natural law has been violated, Nemesis goes into action against those who defied that divine law."

"And how does a mere mortal file a charge with Themis?"

"That is difficult," answered Aristophanes. "Though gods are generally above the law, most behave appropriately, so there is no need to file a charge. But when a god acts inappropriately one must appear before the tribunal on Mount Olympus, and that is next to impossible.

"So what you're saying," said Lisa, "is that our likelihood of getting satisfaction is no better than a snowball's chance in hell. My God, this is worse than fighting City Hall."

"I'm sorry, I don't understand what you are saying."

"Do you know what it means to be up the creek? Well, that's us; up shit creek without a paddle." Lisa's frustration had apparently reached the boiling point.

"I fail to understand your odd phrases."

"What Lisa is trying to say is this: we're distressed that an attempt has been made on our lives, and it appears that nothing can be done about it. We feel helpless and terrified that it may happen again—at any time."

"I understand your concern," said Aristophanes, "but perhaps you should speak directly to Ares. He appears to be the cause of your trouble."

"But Ares is the one who's trying to kill us! How do you propose we deal with him without ending up at the bottom of the Aegean

Sea?" And then it suddenly occurred to me: of course, we will have his girlfriend intercede. Aphrodite is the logical answer to our problem.

And there she was, lovelier than ever, making herself quite at home in our sitting room when we returned to our inn.

"Tell me about your meeting with Socrates," she said. "Was he helpful?"

"Indeed he was," I answered. "But there is a more urgent matter we'd like to discuss. An attempt was made on our lives just as we left Socrates, and the would-be criminals were Deimos and Phobos, twin sons of Ares, we are told."

"I'm shocked to hear that," said Aphrodite. "I must say those boys are a real handful."

"Handful?" cried Lisa. "You think they're a real handful? A colicky baby who won't stop crying is a handful. Ares' sons are goddamned assassins! They're killers who should be locked up!"

"Now calm down, Lisa, I think I can handle this problem. The boys were apparently acting on their father's orders, so we must speak directly to Ares."

"And how do you propose we do that without provoking him further?" I asked.

"Please wait," she answered, "and I will bring Ares here within the hour."

We sat quietly, but after a few minutes Lisa asked, "Do you think we can get away before they return? This is like waiting for the executioner to arrive."

"There's really no place to hide. We have to trust that Aphrodite will protect us."

"This is crazy, George, how the hell did we get into this mess? We may not have the greatest marriage, but the worst thing we ever faced was divorce. Now, it's death by impalement! When will this dreadful nightmare end?"

Before an hour passed Aphrodite returned with our archenemy, who appeared quite different from the last time we were together. His eyes were sunken and red, and his complexion was deathly pale. He seemed to be suffering great discomfort.

"Ares is not well," said Aphrodite, "but he agreed to come here so that we might resolve the problem that exists between you."

"What seems to be the trouble, Ares?" I thought I'd begin with a deferential approach.

"I have a fever, pain between my eyes, and a terrible ache in my head."

"Do you have a runny nose and clogged ears as well?"

"Yes, how did you know?"

I knew because a few years ago I had a bout of sinusitis, including a few painful sinus headaches. It was precisely the symptoms that now seemed to afflict our adversary.

"Well, Ares, you've come to the right place. Wait here a moment and I'll be right back."

I went into our bedchamber, found my toilet kit, and picked up my travel flashlight and two maximum strength sinus pills. I had assembled a collection of travel pills over time, so that if I ever had a migraine, constipation, or a strange itch while in some foreign city, I could avoid seeking out a pharmacy in the middle of the night. I knew from first-hand experience the sinus pills were extremely effective.

"I think I can help you, Ares, but first, I must examine you." This ploy was merely for show, as I wanted our enemy to see my light-emitting-diode flashlight in action. I wanted him to know he wasn't the only person in the room who could perform supernatural tricks. He might be able to turn himself into a wild boar, as he did when he killed Apollo, but, by God, I had an LED flashlight!

"Wait a minute," he said. "Are you a medical person?"

"I suppose so, in a matter of speaking. Actually, I'm an architect; my job is problem solving. And let me say, pal, you have one hell of a problem. You should also know that I greatly admire Apollo, your god of healing, and I once wrote a paper on Hippocrates. Would you care to hear me recite his oath?"

"No, that won't be necessary."

I put my hand on his forehead, as my Beverly Hills internist might do, and shined the powerful beam at his left eye. I had no more idea why my internist did that than Ares did at that very moment. However, it certainly got his attention. "Holy Hades!" he cried, "I'm blinded!"

"Take it easy," I said. "You'll be fine in a moment." Then I examined his other eye. When he seemed the perfect candidate for a seeing-eye dog I turned off the flashlight. Then I put the sinus pills in his hand, poured a cup of water, and ordered him to swallow the pills. "What are these?" he asked. It occurred to me that if I tried to explain the two thousand years of pharmaceutical evolution that led to maximum strength sinus pills, he would probably be asleep before I got to blood-sucking leeches.

"They are magical pills from another age," I said. "They should provide relief in about twenty minutes or so." I then called for Polona and instructed her to bring me a warm, moist cloth. When it arrived I had Ares lie down, and I placed the cloth over his eyes, nose, and entire sinus area. By this time my patient appeared as intimidated as anyone who had ever fallen into the hands of a genuine quack. If I told him to stand on his head and recite lyric poetry by Sappho, I'm sure he would have done so. The only thing missing from my presentation was the white coat, stethoscope; and, of course, the outrageous bill I would never send.

While all this activity was going on, Aphrodite and Lisa sat quietly watching my performance. "I sure hope you know what you're doing," whispered Lisa.

"When it come to sinus headaches, my dear, no one is more expert than I. And if I'm wrong, the power of suggestion will make him believe he had a world-class sinus attack."

About twenty minutes later Ares removed the warm compress, arose, and proclaimed that an absolute miracle had occurred. His fever had broken, he was able to breathe normally, and his aches had significantly diminished. He approached, kneeled in front of me, and kissed my hands.

"You have made me well, and I thank you," he said. "I also wish to apologize for the misunderstanding we had, as well as the exuberance of my sons." Exuberance? How about attempted murder? In any event, along with Ares' painful condition, our personal crisis had just been cured, as if by magic.

"You are quite welcome," I said. "I hope that, from now on you will think twice before using your powers so indiscriminately. Lisa and I meant you no harm, and there was little reason to go to war against us. You are a brave and fearless warrior, Ares, but you are more famously known for being impulsive and bloodthirsty. If your skills could be used for more peaceful purposes you might become more beloved."

"But I am the god of war," he replied. "The very essence of what I do means I will never become beloved. I have always known that. You see, Eirene is the goddess of peace, and I cannot infringe on her powers. I must be the god I was destined to be; I must be true to who I am."

For the first time I began to understand and actually sympathize with Ares. He favored war over peace because that is who he was, and there was no way to modify his behavior. If there were no wars, there would be no Ares. And if I told him that twenty-five hundred years later nothing would change—that terrible wars would still prevail throughout the world, and that peace would remain elusive—he probably would have said, "And that is the simple reason I exist."

NINE

I sat in the brilliant sunshine of our courtyard the next morning, relaxing for the first time in days. Lisa had left to do some shopping at the nearby Agora. "What could you possibly need?" I asked. "You haven't even unpacked your suitcase."

"Don't be so obtuse, George. You know I can't be seen in those modern outfits. Why, I'd be the laughing stock of Athens. Honestly, sometimes I think you spout that nonsense just to annoy me." Not true, I thought; she really didn't need my help. Since landing in ancient Greece she appeared to be perpetually annoyed.

"By the way," I asked, "what will you use for money?"

"I've worked that out with Zoe. She suggested I tell people that I'm a guest at the inn; so send the bills here and she'll settle up with Aphrodite."

"Nice scam," I said.

Lisa ignored the comment and left without another word. And I was left with the usual feelings of despondency. It seemed that efforts to repair our damaged relationship were going nowhere. We had spoken with Aphrodite, received advice from the Delphic Oracle, and visited Socrates, hoping their collective wisdom would lead to an improved marriage. Yet, we seemed no happier now than the day we ran into Doros and his donkey. Where do we go from here, I wondered? And is it possible our problem has no solution? What a depressing thought that was.

So there I sat in our sunny courtyard, with *Bullfinch's Mythology* on my lap and a handful of walnuts beside me for snacking. Though I remained skeptical of Socrates' cure for asthenospermia, I enjoyed walnuts and figured they could do little harm.

I planned to read some mythological love stories, hopeful that a solution for our relationship might be lurking among those ancient gems. But where to begin? Love was one of the most popular mythological topics, and whether it was inspired, unrequited, or forbidden, it was a vital part of ancient Greek existence.

I began with the story of Eros and Psyche. Eros, the deity of love and passion, was portrayed as a handsome young adult with wings, ever-present bow, and love-tinged arrows. Psyche was a mortal princess whose extraordinary beauty incurred the jealousy of Aphrodite. Thus, the envious goddess ordered Eros to make her fall in love with the most hideous creature on earth. However, when Eros saw the sleeping Psyche he fell hopelessly in love and spirited her away to his home. He visited her only after dark, since he wanted to keep his identity unknown and be certain she would love him as an equal, rather than a god. Thus, she had no clue to his appearance.

Psyche's sisters, believing that Eros might actually be a monster, convinced her to spy on him while he slept. Carrying an oil lamp into the room she discovered that Eros was not a monster, but a youth more beautiful than she had ever seen. While putting out the lamp a drop of hot oil fell on Eros' shoulder. He awoke, and flew out the window exclaiming, "Love cannot live where there is suspicion." For several years Psyche wandered the earth, searching for Eros. Eventually, Aphrodite took pity on her, made Psyche immortal, and allowed the couple to marry.

It was a happy ending, I suppose, but those years apart didn't sound all that wonderful. Nevertheless, it was far happier than the following myth.

Hero and Leander were lovers who lived on opposite sides of the Hellespont. At nightfall Hero would hang a lantern so Leander could swim across to her, using the light to guide him. One stormy night the wind blew out the light, and Leander lost his way and drowned. Upon learning of her lover's death, Hero drowned herself in order to be with him at the bottom of the sea.

And if you think that's depressing, read on.

Pyramus and Thisbe were lovers who met each night at a spot outside the city. One evening Thisbe arrived early but fled when she saw a lion approaching. In her haste she dropped her cloak. The lion, fresh from a hunt, mauled the cloak with its bloodstained paws and retreated. When Pyramus arrived and saw the bloodstained cloak he assumed the worst. In anguish, he plunged a deadly knife into his heart. Thisbe later found his body and, in desperation, also killed herself, rather than live without the love of her life.

Yes, I know it sounds a lot like *Romeo and Juliet*. A person comes upon the dead lover and—overcome by grief—commits suicide. It's a terrible tragedy, but what's with all these suicides? Why are surviving lovers so ready to kill themselves? Would I jump off the Golden Gate Bridge if Lisa died? Not very likely. And would Lisa put rat poison in her tea if I were run over by a bus? Are you kidding? Living unhappily without your partner is an awful fate, but suicide doesn't sound like much fun either. As far as I'm concerned, killing yourself because of love is no more rational than killing yourself because of hate—as suicide bombers do with amazing regularity.

A somewhat happier ending characterizes the following myth. Philemon and Baucis were an elderly couple who lived a simple life in a small village. One day Hermes and Zeus, disguised as weary travelers, came to their village to test the hospitality of the citizens. It was that same filoxenia issue Lisa and I experienced on our first night in Athens. The two travelers were treated ungraciously by nearly all, until they reached the modest home of Philemon and Baucis. There they found a cozy home and were offered every comfort the humble couple could provide. Dropping their disguises, the gods revealed their true identities and offered to grant any wish the old couple might have. Their simple request was to die at the same moment, so they may never be apart. Many years later, as they both began to fade away, they kissed, said their last farewells, and were transformed into trees—an oak and a linden— whose boughs were intertwined, symbolizing their everlasting love.

What a beautiful end! No doubt every loving couple would prefer to die together. Consider the advantages: You need not mourn for your partner, nor is either one condemned to live alone or forced to contemplate suicide. No doubt about it, Philemon and Baucis got it exactly right. By contrast, the story of Orpheus and Eurydice had an awful ending.

Orpheus, an extremely gifted musician, was in love with the fair maiden, Eurydice. As luck would have it, on their wedding day she stepped on a poisonous snake, died instantly, and ended up in the underworld. Because his music charmed the gods, Orpheus was allowed to enter the underworld to visit his beloved. He was even allowed to take Eurydice back with him, provided he did not look at her before reaching the land of the living. Unfortunately, Orpheus became anxious, glanced back to be sure Eurydice was there, and she was immediately sent back to Hades' realm forever. Orpheus spent his rest of his days wandering in aimless sorrow.

This myth was probably a warning to young Greeks that ignoring rules has serious consequences. The following myth also shows the great unhappiness love can cause.

Narcissus was an extremely handsome youth who was shocked by the sight of his reflection in a pool of water. Never having seen himself before, he believed the reflection was someone else, someone with whom he became absolutely enchanted. He remained by the pool for weeks and never lost his love for the reflection. Some said he died from lack of nourishment; others believed he killed himself with his own dagger when he realized he had fallen in love with his reflection. Either way, ancient Greeks showed little tolerance for excessive self-love.

A story of forbidden love was that of Jocasta and Oedipus. Oedipus was abandoned by his parents at birth and raised by a shepherd. As an adult he traveled to Thebes, where he solved an age-old riddle, and by so doing received the throne of the city and the hand in marriage of the widowed queen, Jocasta. Neither realized that Jocasta was actually Oedipus's mother. Despite the age difference, the marriage was successful and enduring. Later, however, when they discovered their true relationship Jocasta committed suicide, and Oedipus blinded himself and went into exile.

My afternoon ended with the unique story of Pygmalion and Galatea. Pygmalion was a gifted sculptor who was unable to find a woman worthy of his love. He dedicated himself to his work and began to create in marble the perfect woman he suspected he would never find. He called the statue Galatea, and after many months of work there stood before him a female form of such exquisite beauty and unrivaled perfection that he fell deeply in love with it.

Pygmalion went to the temple of Aphrodite, and prayed to the goddess of love to bring his work of art to life. When he returned home his statue seemed oddly warm to the touch. Then he kissed her lips and discovered they were soft and moist. He stood back to regard the statue and noticed a glow of life within the marble form. Was he imagining all this? No, Aphrodite had given life to Galatea, and thus, the story had the happiest of all possible endings.

So, what—if anything—did I learn from these ancient myths? First, I was greatly impressed by the intensity of those loving relationships. These were no mere flings, but rather legends of powerful passion and devotion. Equally remarkable was the emphasis on sex. It occurred to me that Pygmalion could not have cared less if Galatea was a total nincompoop; essentially, it was all about sex. I also noticed that it was only after dark that Eros visited Psyche, Leander swam to Hero, and Pyramus met Thisbe. Why after dark? What were they doing in the dark? Discussing politics? Of course not. They were making love; it was all about sex. They were screwing their mythological brains out!

And then it hit me; that is exactly what we were missing. Lisa and I had many problems, but our most critical one was the total lack of sex. How dense could I have been? I never realized until now that our bickering was anger over a sexless relationship and a pathetic substitute for intimacy. But what could I do about it? Speak to Lisa? Good God, no. She would reject the notion and claim I was simply obsessed with sex. How about Aphrodite? Should I discuss this with her? After all, she's the goddess of love, desire, and all things sexual. If she can't solve this problem, then what's the point of having a goddess of love? That's it, I thought, I will talk to Aphrodite.

Having spent the last few hours reading, I now felt the need for a stroll. I headed towards the Agora with the notion that I might bump into Lisa along the way. Instead, I immediately ran into Aristophanes, the Good Samaritan who saved us from the reckless sons of Ares.

"Hello, George," he greeted me. "You're looking quite relaxed today. Have you settled your problems with Ares, as I suggested?"

"Yes indeed, that was a valuable piece of advice, for which I thank you. We ironed out our differences, and he has become one of my biggest fans."

"How so?"

"Well, he was suffering from a terrible sinus attack, and I was able to relieve his discomfort. He's now convinced I can perform medical magic."

"Can you?"

"Not really, but don't tell Ares."

"Never fear, it shall remain our secret. By the way, there will be a performance of my play this afternoon. Would you and your wife care to attend?"

"You know, when we met I thought your name sounded familiar, but I didn't recall that you were a playwright. We would be honored to attend." He gave me information about the performance, and I promised we'd meet after the show. I found Lisa back at our room a short time later, and she was thrilled to hear about our invitation to the play. "How wonderful!" she said. "I'm beginning to feel like part of Athens' social elite."

"Take it easy, it's only a play, not a command performance on Mount Olympus."

The Theater of Dionysus, named for the patron god of drama, was located in a natural hollow on the south slope of the Acropolis. It was a huge theater, perhaps the size of the Hollywood Bowl, and like the Bowl it was open to the sky. The form of the theater was a semi-circle, in which tiers of seats rose from the circular orchestra to the rear rows. Our seats were down front, close to the action.

The title of Aristophanes' play was *Lysistrata*, a classic play I had heard of, but about which I knew little. It turned out to be an entertaining anti-war drama with a decidedly sexual theme. The play's star, Lysistrata, is a spirited young woman who is determined to end the Peloponnesian War. The conflict between Athens and Sparta has been going on for years, and women have become tired of politics, warfare, and losing their men in battle. Her plan is to meet with wives and lovers from both sides and convince them to withhold sex from their men until both sides agree to sign a peace treaty. The women reluctantly swear an oath of agreement. Lysistrata also makes plans with the older women of Athens to seize the treasury at the Acropolis, so that the Athenians no longer have funds to wage war.

After a week without sex the chaste women, who are barricaded at the Acropolis, become restless and are tempted to break their oath. Lysistrata convinces them that the men are suffering even more severely, so they should be patient. In fact, several of the husbands approach the women, with the illusion of gigantic erections, in order to plead their case. But they are turned away. At this point, Lisa and I were glued to our seats. Eventually, a Spartan, also with a fake erection about the size of a stallion, approaches the Parthenon, describes the desperate sexual situation in Sparta, and pleads for a treaty. An agreement is reached, Lysistrata gives the women back to the men, and a great celebration follows.

The play was a fantasy, of course. Athenian women were clearly second-class citizens, unable to vote or have much control over their lives. But Aristophanes' skill was portraying women as brilliant negotiators who go on a sex strike to end a war. Making love, not war, was a total reversal of societal norms. It was also the most entertaining hour and a half we enjoyed since arriving in ancient Athens.

When we caught up with Aristophanes, a crowd of well-wishers surrounded him.

"Wonderful play!" I said. "I'm so grateful for your invitation."

"Me, too," said Lisa. "I haven't enjoyed theater this much since *A Midsummer Night's Dream*."

"I'm afraid I don't know that," said Aristophanes.

"It's not important," I said. "It won't matter for another two thousand years."

He gave me a perplexed look and then said, "Several of us are going to a nearby tavern to celebrate. Will you join us?"

When we arrived, wine was flowing freely, and everyone was talking about *Lysistrata*. "What I don't understand," said an elderly man to Aristophanes "is why you portrayed women capable of taking over a city and ending a war. That seems so utterly implausible."

"I don't think it's implausible at all," interrupted Lisa. "Women may be the weaker sex, but they can do nearly everything men can do; and actually, some things they do much better."

"Excuse me," said the man. "We haven't been introduced. My name is Andro, and I must say your notions are quite eccentric. Are you a citizen of Athens?"

"No, Andro, I am a visitor. My name is Lisa, and I come from a place very far from here. But it is a place where women are treated with the same deference as men. I have female friends who are professors, architects, civic leaders, and all enjoy as much freedom as Athenian men."

"Extraordinary!" said Andro. "What a strange place that must be."

"I, too, find it strange," said Aristophanes. "But how interesting to know that what I imagined could truly come to pass. Total equality of men and women has always been a fantasy."

"Not on Mount Olympus," said Lisa. "How do you account for the power of goddesses like Athena, Hera, or Aphrodite? Aren't they equal in stature to Apollo, Ares, and Poseidon?"

"I suppose you have a point," said Aristophanes.

"Let's change the subject," I said to Lisa. "I don't think this celebration should turn into a feminist rally. Remember, we're guests here."

"You're being sexist, George."

"Oh please, you know me better than that."

We had a few drinks, made small talk with several other guests, and by then the party had run its course. We walked back to our inn and fell into bed.

"I'm proud of you, Lisa." I said. "I liked the way you stood up for women, and I think you expressed your views with appropriate passion."

"Are you being sarcastic?"

"Not at all. That was a genuine complement."

"Goodnight, George." It was apparently the end of the conversation.

I suddenly thought about Aphrodite and the subject very much on my mind—sex. I was beginning to feel like those sexually disenfranchised warriors in Aristophanes' play. I've got to talk to her, I thought. And the sooner the better.

TEN

I saw Aphrodite early the following morning. "Can we talk?" I asked.

"Certainly, George. What's on your mind?

We sat on the bench beneath the olive tree in our courtyard just as the sun was peeking over the surrounding walls. It was a typically radiant morning. "I think I know what's behind much of our problem," I began. "In a nutshell, it's the utter lack of sex. There doesn't seem to be a shred of affection left in this marriage. Forget the bickering and sarcasm, forget the hostility; we don't even touch any more. And the last time we kissed was a year ago on New Year's Eve. Honest to God, I get more sexual pleasure from flirting with the checkout girl at the supermarket than I get at home. How can there be any love when there's absolutely no physical expression of that love?"

"You are right, of course. It is the same thought I've had for a long time. You two have not been living as a married couple for much too long. However, I have an idea that may correct that situation. Let us meet this afternoon, and I shall outline my plan to you both."

"If it involves us jumping into bed together, save your breath. Lisa will surely reject that notion."

"Trust me, George. I am the goddess of love; I know what I'm doing."

When I told Lisa that Aphrodite had proposed a meeting with us that afternoon to discuss our next therapeutic move she was immediately suspicious.

"What's this all about?" she asked.

"I have no idea. I only know that she has a plan, which she will describe to us."

"Are you cooking up something to upset me?"

"Not at all; I know nothing more than I've told you. Anyway, what's your choice? Do you want to repair this marriage or not? If you want to quit right now we could get a quickie Athenian divorce and go our separate ways."

"Are you threatening me?"

"Yes, I suppose I am. I've just about had enough of your negative attitude and lack of concern for us. Here's a chance to consider what the goddess of love suggests and you're searching for an evil plot. You have a choice, Lisa: either we listen to the expert and move forward, or count me out. I'm not playing this game any longer."

The three of us met in our sitting room that afternoon. Despite the dismal level of our relationship I actually felt optimistic. Lisa, on the other hand appeared deeply depressed, and despite our differences, I felt genuine sympathy for her.

"I have devised an exercise for you two," began Aphrodite, "that I believe will shed light on your relationship. This exercise involves sexual relations, and it is meant to be therapeutic. Neither of you has been with a sexual partner for a long time; thus, we hope to discover what part that might play in the difficulties affecting your relationship. I have selected partners for you both, neither of whom has a personal interest in you. They are merely surrogates for the purpose of this experiment."

"Are you suggesting we have sex with total strangers?" asked Lisa.

"That is exactly what I am suggesting," answered Aphrodite.

"I'm not sure I can do that," Lisa said. "I feel a certain loyalty to George, and this would be contrary to everything our marriage has stood for."

"But currently, your marriage doesn't stand for much. There is little affection, a total absence of sexual activity, and considerable ill will. So what exactly does your loyalty represent?"

Lisa considered that for a moment and then asked, "Would I be able to see my partner?"

"No, the room will be totally dark and you will both be blindfolded. Neither of you will be able to see one another. But I can tell you this: I have chosen your partners carefully, and they are both quite attractive. You will respond to the senses of smell, taste, and touch, but not vision or sound, for you are forbidden to speak to one another. I think you will enjoy this experience; it will be gentle, pleasurable, and enlightening."

"What do you think about this, George?" asked Lisa. "Do you favor this so-called exercise?"

"I believe Aphrodite has thought this through, and if she thinks this will help, I'm all for it."

"This wouldn't have anything to do with having a little guilt-free sex, would it?"

"I'll try to feel guilty, if that will make you feel better."

"You are missing the point," said Aphrodite. "This exercise should be free of guilt for you both. The purpose is for you to enjoy the physical pleasure of lovemaking, without emotional connections. It will free you from the constraints that have damaged your relationship, and my hope is that you will become sexually liberated so you can, once again, find love for one another."

"So how will this work?" asked Lisa.

"You will be in separate rooms, and you will be aware when you and your partner meet. You are encouraged to respond to your partner's advances and do what comes naturally. You may do anything that brings you pleasure, but you may not speak. Do you both understand the rules of this experiment?"

Lisa and I nodded, and I noticed she wore a half smile. As for me, I could hardly wait to meet my surrogate.

Later that evening the house slaves, Polona and Thea, bathed us and rubbed us with sweet smelling lotions. I felt like a gladiator being prepared for battle, but in this case, it appeared, every contestant would be a winner and live to tell the grandchildren about it.

How can I describe the indescribable pleasure of that evening? It was so beyond my wildest fantasies and incredible expectations, I am nearly without words. Let me first say that before Lisa there were a few memorable experiences with other women. Some I remember quite fondly. But when Lisa came along she nearly erased from memory anyone before her. She was the absolute personification of sexual delight. She always knew precisely what to do and how to do it in order to bring us the greatest satisfaction. I truly believed no partner would ever surpass the skill, dexterity, and tenderness of my very own Lisa. But that evening with my surrogate made me question that belief.

Polona applied my blindfold and then guided me to the assigned room where my surrogate lay waiting. I was guided to the bed and then I heard the door to the room shut. I sat on the edge of the bed and tried to get my bearings. I reached out and immediately felt the bare flesh of an arm. It was smooth, soft, and warm. As a blind man might do, I followed the curve of the arm, like a road map, until I reached a shoulder. It is amazing what thoughts occur to those who are sightless. I was certain the curve of this shoulder was as beautifully proportioned and visually perfect as the finest sculpture I had ever seen.

When I touched the shoulder, her body turned slightly in my direction. My hand next traced a route downward until I reached a bare breast. It was modest in size, but as full and firm and soft to the touch as the loveliest breast one could only imagine in a fantasy. When I ran my hand over the breast I felt her body tremble ever so slightly. We had just begun this marvelous experiment, but I found the preliminary activity incredibly arousing.

I next moved onto the bed and stretched out parallel to my partner. I lifted myself onto an elbow and lowered my head to kiss her on the forehead. From there I moved slowly south, planting soft kisses on her ear, cheek, neck, and finally her mouth. Her lips were slightly apart, and I took the opportunity to explore that intimate area. I then moved to her breast, where I continued planting soft kisses. I began to feel totally unrestrained and reckless. Why not, I thought, she's my surrogate; she's here to provide pleasure, not to grade my performance. Let's just have fun and enjoy ourselves. After all, it's been a long time coming. I chuckled silently at my choice of words.

My partner turned toward me and put an arm around my neck. Then I felt her warm breath only inches from my face. She moved forward and grazed my lips with hers before returning to kiss me deeply and with great passion. I felt her body down below, and my touch produced a shudder that seemed to travel like an electric current from her head to toes. I sensed she was ready to consummate our encounter. I slowly entered and was surprised by the passionate response. She seemed equally as thrilled as I to be joined as one, and what an incredible thrill it was!

We completed the act in a short time and then lay in each other's arms, breathing like two runners who had just completed a marathon. An overwhelming feeling of peace and contentment enveloped me. It was a feeling I had not experienced for a very long time. She, too, seemed relaxed and quite content. After a short while she moved her body on top of me and became the aggressor. She held my arms above my head and attacked me with well-aimed kisses. It didn't take long before we were ready to resume our lovemaking. She placed me inside of her and set the pace of our movements. It was incredibly erotic and deeply satisfying. When she finally collapsed on my chest we were totally exhausted and completely satisfied. It had been an extraordinary experience.

What do I do now? I wanted to express my gratitude and delight, but we were warned not to make a sound. So I turned to my partner, found her lips, and gave her a tender kiss. Let her interpret that as she will, I thought. I was saying, "thank you for this memorable experience". I stood up, prepared to leave, but where was the door? I moved to the foot of the bed, stretched out an arm, and felt the wooden door. I rapped on it and Polona reached out to grab my hand. "This way," she said. She removed my blindfold and the dim light made me wince. "You will see normally in just a few moments," she said.

I put on a robe, and we returned to our sitting room where Aphrodite apparently waited for our report. I poured a glass of wine and took a seat. "Lisa should be here soon," she said, "so let us wait before we speak of your experience." I sat quietly, sipping my wine and recalling every erotic moment of my incredible adventure. I had no idea what it would prove, but at the moment, it didn't really matter. What did matter was my realization that sexual pleasure was an important part of my life, and that aspect of our marriage had been sorely missed.

As Lisa entered the room she appeared to glow like a radiant blossom. Her cheeks were flushed, and her entire body moved as though she were gliding on ice skates. She took a seat, looked in my direction, and nodded at me with the sweetest smile I had ever seen.

"I assume your experience was pleasurable," suggested Aphrodite.

"So much so," answered Lisa, "I feel terribly guilty about George."

"And you, George," asked Aphrodite, "how was your experience?"

"It did produce a certain guilt," I answered. "After all, I take my marital vows seriously, but I must admit this sexual event was beyond any erotic fantasy I ever had. I only regret that it was not Lisa with whom I shared this exciting moment."

"I had the same thought," said Lisa. "Why couldn't this be George I asked myself? I'm sure, if he felt so inclined, he could bring me as much pleasure as I just experienced. It was, without a doubt, the most erotically satisfying encounter I've ever had."

"So," said Aphrodite, "the experiment was successful, certainly in its sexual aspect, but what have you learned about each other?"

"I learned that I deeply miss the sexual Lisa—the way we used to be."

"And I, too, miss the physical relationship we used to enjoy," said Lisa. There was a long pause during which a quizzical expression formed on Lisa's face. "Could you, by any chance, reveal the identities of our partners this evening?" she asked.

"I suppose it would do little harm now," said Aphrodite. "As difficult as it may be to accept this answer, the sexual partners you both enjoyed this evening . . . were you!"

I sat there dumbstruck for a moment. "You mean my partner—the person with whom I had the greatest erotic moment of my life—was Lisa?"

"Yes," answered Aphrodite.

"This isn't some kind of joke, is it?" asked Lisa.

"No, it may have been a trick, but it was certainly not a joke. Your partner was you're husband, George."

We sat there quietly for a long time contemplating the meaning of Aphrodite's experiment. Was it possible that two people who were at odds with one another, virtual adversaries—so to speak—and openly hostile at times, could these same two people share the greatest sexual encounter of their lives? Well, I suppose it was possible, because it apparently just happened.

Why, I wondered, didn't I recognize Lisa by the touch of her hand, the taste of her kiss, or the smell of her hair? I can only suppose it was the way the experiment was originally presented—that we would be with unknown surrogates who were faceless strangers. That made it inconceivable to imagine we were with our own spouses. It was a clever trick, and it worked. But now what? Could one night of sexual pleasure erase years of hostility? I had no idea.

"Well," said Lisa, "no reason to feel guilty, is there?"

"Not at all," I said. "Only grateful to each other for a wonderful experience."

"Here is what I hoped you would learn from this," said Aphrodite. "You two may have lost your way, but you have much that binds you, sexual pleasure being only the most obvious reason you are well suited. For a short while tonight you expressed to each other a most exceptional form of love. Without recognizing your partner you gave of yourselves to bring pleasure to another. This is the very basis of a successful relationship— offering pleasure unselfishly to another. You must use that principle to rebuild the relationship you once enjoyed. I am certain you can do that."

Aphrodite left the room and we retired to our bedchamber. We both felt a bit self-conscious; after months of unemotional behavior we had shared a deeply personal experience. Things were not the same, and we both realized it. But what exactly were they? As we lay in our bed, Lisa touched my hand.

"You were magnificent tonight, George."

"And you, my dear, you were an absolute goddess."

Our relationship had definitely improved, and I was convinced it would only get better.

ELEVEN

It was still dark when I awoke early the next morning. I had dreamed of an odd but wonderful sexual encounter. I did not recognize my partner, but I remained in a half stupor savoring the details. I figured the dream was prompted by the extraordinary events of the previous night. I reached out to Lisa, with the hope we might pick up where we left off. There were occasions in our earlier years when I awoke in the middle of the night and put an arm around her, which often led to lovemaking. Even when she was half asleep, Lisa never failed to join in with enthusiasm. She was incredibly generous and loving.

Referring to me as the Midnight Marauder, she once asked, "Why do you save your best for the middle of the night?"

"I can't explain it," I would say. "I suppose I feel at ease, I think of that sensual body lying just inches away, and I can't control myself."

"I'm not complaining, mind you; I'm just curious. You know, you don't have to sneak up on me at night. I love you, and I'm available to you anytime—day or night."

As I reached out, I felt nothing; Lisa was not in our bed. Could she be in the toilet room? I waited five minutes and then got out of bed. I checked the toilet room, but no one was there. Could she have gone for a walk? I didn't think she would leave the inn without telling me; it was not like her to do that. But who knows? I got dressed, went outside, and walked as far as the Agora. There was no Lisa. I was becoming uneasy; where could she be?

I decided to see Zoe. "You're up early, George. Is there anything wrong?"

"I hope not, but Lisa has disappeared. Or at least, I can't find her."

"I'll have Polona and Thea search the grounds; she couldn't have gone far." The two household slaves searched for about twenty minutes, but they found no trace of Lisa. However, they did find a herald's wand, which was a short staff entwined by two serpents.

"I think this is Herme's wand," said Zoe. "How very unusual."

"Hermes?" I said. "Messenger of the gods, guardian of wayfarers, the same guy who visited us our first night here?"

"Yes," answered Zoe. "I believe Hermes was here, and I suspect your Lisa has gone off with him."

"What do you mean gone off with him? If she's with him, she didn't go willingly. Lisa would never disappear without a word. I'm sure she's been kidnapped."

"She may have been half asleep," suggested Zoe, "or perhaps he was wearing his Cap of Invisibility. In that case she may not have known who carried her away. On the other hand, perhaps our worries are unnecessary. You know, Hermes is known as a trickster and mischief-maker. It's possible he's just having a bit of fun."

"Fun? What kind of degenerate thinks kidnapping is fun?"

"Calm down, George. We'll get to the bottom of this. I'll contact Aphrodite; she'll know what to do."

Aphrodite arrived within the hour. "What bad luck, George. Just when I thought we were making progress, along comes Hermes to cause trouble. I saw him this morning and Lisa was with him. She looked confused and unhappy. She may have enjoyed the flight to Mount Olympus, but her presence has angered the gods. You see, mortals are not permitted to visit the Olympian home. So there she is, uncomfortable to be an object of scorn."

"Did she say anything about returning here?"

"No, but I suppose that will be up to Hermes."

"That's little consolation. The last time we ran into that prankster there was a mild flirtation going on. I didn't trust him then, and I certainly don't trust him now. What's with you Greek gods? Is sex all you think about?"

"You are asking the wrong person. I am—after all—the goddess of love and procreation. Of course sex is an essential part of my existence, but I have other interests as well. However, if you assume Hermes took Lisa for the purpose of lovemaking, I suspect you are wrong."

"Why else would he kidnap my wife in the middle of the night?"

"As I said, Hermes was probably having fun, making a bit of mischief."

"Well, if we ever meet again I'll show that sociopath some real mischief."

I felt angry and helpless; my poor Lisa was being held captive by a psychotic god, who just happened to be young, gorgeous, and in possession of more magical tricks than Houdini. He could fly through the air, make himself invisible, and the inconsiderate son-of-a-bitch was immortal! As if that weren't enough, his father was Zeus, the king of all gods! How in the world could I possibly compete with someone who had such an incredible résumé?

I thought about that for a long time and finally concluded there was a way; I would have to outwit him. I needed a plan that would pit my twenty-first century intellect against his Olympian powers. But how? He seemed to be holding all the cards. Then it suddenly came to me; I will make Lisa appear so hazardous, so serious a risk to his well being, that he'll be delighted to drop her like a hot potato. As the plan formed in my mind I said to Aphrodite, "I must go to Mount Olympus to see Hermes and rescue my wife."

"Very noble, George, but that's impossible. Mortals are not allowed there."

"Well, what the hell is Lisa doing up there?"

"Incurring the wrath of all the other gods. She will not be there very long, I assure you."

"Then it is imperative that I see Hermes here. You must tell him he is in grave danger."

"Are you certain about this?"

"I am, and he will be grateful forever for what I am about to tell him."

Aphrodite appeared convinced and said, "I don't think he will allow Lisa to return with him, but he and I shall be back here very shortly." I figured that would give me plenty of time to do a bit of research and prepare my presentation.

After Aphrodite's departure I went to our room and began making notes. I kept thinking about Hermes and his outsized ego. He was known as a trickster who outwitted other gods for his own satisfaction. Could I turn the tables and outwit the cunning bastard? Would he accept the facts I was about to describe? If my story was outrageous enough I thought he would.

"So what's this all about?" asked Hermes. He appeared cheerful and as arrogant as ever. "I suppose borrowing your wife without your permission has you a bit on edge."

"That doesn't bother me nearly as much as recognizing the incredible danger you're in. You see, Hermes, there is much you do not know about my good wife. Her health is precarious, and the longer you are around her the greater your risk. For example, have you ever heard of the condition called *ichthyocolitis*? Only a few people who have come in contact with Lisa have been afflicted, so perhaps you need not worry. But let me describe the symptoms. It generally begins with an itch in your groin; you know what I mean—the kind of itch that endless scratching cannot satisfy. Then the itch migrates to your scalp. You scratch, your hair begins to thin, and one day you are suddenly and completely bald. Believe me, ichthyocolitis is no picnic."

I thought I'd begin with his most cherished assets, his crotch and his incredibly full head of lustrous black hair. Happily, it seemed to work; I had his undivided attention. Better yet, he seemed completely unaware that ichthyocolitis was a condition I borrowed from an old Danny Kaye movie, a condition known to affect only fresh water fish.

"There's more, Hermes, much more.

"What more could there be?" he asked.

"Well, let's talk about sexual relations. I assume that is what attracted you to Lisa in the first place. Am I correct?"

"Well, I suppose. She *is* attractive," he admitted.

"How far have you gone with that idea?"

"Not very far. Before she awoke from our trip to Mount Olympus, I kissed her."

"Where?"

"On the lips."

"Oh my goodness; that is *very* bad news."

"Why? What do you mean?"

"I guess you haven't heard of *cryptosporidiosis*. Let me describe that affliction. First of all, one transmits that disease through kissing. If untreated, the result can be oral sores and painful gums. A few days later your teeth become loose, and eventually, they fall out."

"Is there a cure for that?" he asked nervously.

"Stay right here. I may have an antidote for you."

I went to our sleeping chamber, found my toilet kit, and took out small tube of Blistex. I always carried Blistex, because it was an effective cure for chapped lips. I put a small amount on Hermes finger and directed him to spread it on his lips. After a few moments he said, "It feels better already. I don't know how to thank you." The aroma of camphor and menthol was unmistakable, but I'd be shocked if Blistex cured cryptosporidiosis, which was a nasty parasite found in swine. I also doubted it would cure Greek gods who acted like sexual pigs.

"I must say, Hermes, you are one lucky son-of-a-bitch. If you had gone beyond that one kiss there would be no recourse. And even though you can be a horse's ass at times, I doubt that you deserve that kind of trouble."

"To tell the truth," he replied, "I would have gone further, but Lisa claimed she had a terrible headache." Imagine my surprise.

"Well, be happy she did have a headache, because the other condition you should know about concerns actual intercourse, and the affects of that might have spelled the end of you."

"How so?" asked the Olympian trickster.

"Have you ever heard of *dionaea muscipula*? It's also known as the Venus flytrap."

"What is that?"

"It is a highly treacherous carnivorous plant found in sub-tropical areas. When an insect, like a spider, crawls along the leaf of that plant the trap snaps shut and the insect is done for. It takes only a fraction of a second for the insect to be trapped, and the plant digests the poor bastard it in a few days. It's not a pretty sight; all that remains is a blot where the insect was."

"What has that to do with Lisa?"

"Hold on to your chair, Hermes; this might just shiver your timbers. As remarkable as it sounds, Lisa has a vagina like a Venus flytrap. Once you are inside her, there is no escape, and your formerly flawless member is totally consumed and digested in about a half hour. And the pain can only be described as excruciating!"

"I don't believe that."

"Are you willing to risk the integrity of your pecker to prove me wrong?"

"What if one withdraws after a moment or two?"

"Good question. Here's what to expect: If you escape the *Jaws of Death*, as others have described it, your penis will turn black after an hour or so, and it will shrivel to a fraction of its original size. Eventually, the pathetic remains simply fall off."

Hermes sat there quietly digesting what he had just heard. His legs were crossed in anguish, his mouth formed a pained expression, and beads of perspiration covered his forehead.

"I better think this over," he said. "The risks sound greater than the reward."

"Wise decision, Hermes. Remember, he who fights and runs away may live to fight another day. Also, discretion is the better part of valor."

Since I was running out of clichés and my arguments seemed convincing, there was little more to say. Hermes rose and said, "I shall return with your wife shortly."

"No rush, Hermes. Take your time."

"I would be more comfortable having her off Mount Olympus as soon as possible. But first, let me ask a question. Why did you marry a woman with so many terrifying problems?"

"Who can explain why one falls in love? Since the day we were married we have searched for ways to cure her conditions. I am confident we will live a normal life one day; but until that day arrives we remain patient and—perhaps you find will this odd—very much in love."

"I wish you well," said Hermes, "and I am truly sorry for causing you concern."

With his apology, Hermes was off to fetch Lisa. It had been a satisfying afternoon and I could not wait to see my wife again. As for Hermes, if I never saw him again I would consider that a gift from the gods.

Lisa returned within the hour and immediately collapsed into my arms. "You have no idea what I've been through," she said. "I thought I'd never escape that oversexed creep."

"I thought you found him attractive."

"Maybe from a distance, but not when he's drooling right in your face. What on earth did you say that convinced him to release me? He couldn't wait to get me off his hands. He acted as if I carried the plague."

"I told him if he didn't release you at once, I would beat the crap out of him."

"I don't believe that for a second, but it doesn't matter; you are my hero."

"Tell me, what is life like on Mount Olympus? Few mortals have had that experience."

"I promise to tell you everything tomorrow, but I'm totally exhausted and have to sleep right now. I was up all night defending my virtue. I'm ready to collapse."

"Okay, but something else you should know; I was seriously worried about you and I'm really happy you're back where you belong. I guess I discovered just how much I care about you when I thought I might never see you again."

"That goes double for me," she replied.

TWELVE

Lisa remained in an undisturbed sleep for twelve hours. Her ordeal with Hermes had sapped every ounce of physical and emotional strength. When she arose we moved to our sitting room, where we had our usual breakfast of bread, goat cheese, figs, and, of course, walnuts.

"What an adventure that must have been," I said. "I thought you'd sleep until tomorrow."

"I felt like it, but twelve hours on my bag of leaves was enough."

"Now, tell me about Mount Olympus. Since mortals are not allowed there your trip was not only rare, but dangerous as well. Did you ever hear about Bellerophon? He was a mortal who borrowed Pegasus one day and flew to Mount Olympus. That bit of chutzpah so annoyed Zeus he caused Pegasus to throw off Bellerophon, who survived the fall but was crippled for life—and all because the gods were offended by his arrogance."

"First of all, I could have lived very happily without that trip. And my being there had nothing to do with arrogance. It had only to do with that conceited psychopath, Hermes. Since he took me directly to his palace, nobody even knew I was there. But there I stayed until he suddenly decided I was about as desirable as a case of syphilis."

"So, what was it like?"

"It was mostly frightening. I had no idea what he planned to do, but I was sure it was something I wouldn't like. The entrance to Mount

Olympus is a gate of clouds, but I didn't see that until we left. I was unconscious all the way there. The place is home to the dozen most important gods, and each has an individual palace. Hephaestus, who is the god of artisans, built all the palaces; but let me tell you, he's no Ictinus. In fact, in a million years he will never be as good an architect as you are right now. He knows nothing about design; everything is incredibly overwrought. Honest to God, it's worse than the Persian Palaces you see in Beverly Hills."

"Were you offered anything to eat?"

"That was another revelation. You've heard of ambrosia and nectar, the food of the gods? What a joke that is! Ambrosia is a mixture of honey, fruit, cheese and barley; and it tastes worse than it sounds. Nectar is fermented honey, and frankly, I'll take a Coke any day."

"I suppose you know that if you ate enough of that stuff you might live forever. According to legend, ambrosia and nectar allow the gods to remain ageless and immortal."

"That's probably because perpetual diarrhea keeps their systems purified."

"Was there anything you liked about Mount Olympus?"

"Sure, the weather; it's idyllic. It never rains or snows, the breezes are pleasant, and the temperature is always perfect. You might say," she began to smile, "it's a little bit of heaven."

"Very funny. Now, what about the other gods? Did you meet any of them?"

"No, I saw a few, but they're not a particularly friendly bunch. They wander about gossiping and pontificating. Being a god comes with a lot of pressure; they must know everything about their specialties. For example, Poseidon is the god of the seas, so he knows everything there is to know about that; but like most gods, he can be a bit arrogant. So when I heard him giving advice to Dionysus, god of the vine and fertility, I figured he was overstepping his area of expertise. Zeus apparently agreed. As Poseidon became more pompous, Zeus stepped in and told him to mind his own business. 'Stick to what you know,' he said. 'I can assure you, you know nothing about wine!' There's also some jealousy and envy among the gods. In that respect they appear much like mortals. And sex is very much on everyone's mind. There's a lot of talk about it, and in my opinion, they're a pretty randy bunch."

"Well, I'm glad the experience is over, and you're safely home again."

"Thank you, George, I'm touched by your concern."

"It was more than concern; I was worried sick. I wasn't sure if I'd see you again, and the thought of living life without you was pretty depressing."

"Even after all we've been through?"

"Yes, even after all we've been through. Despite the ups and downs, there is something special between us. It's something worthwhile, and something I hope we can salvage. If I didn't believe that, I would have looked the other way and let Hermes have his way with you."

"Well thank you for not looking the other way. Really, I appreciate that."

Thea suddenly entered our sitting room and announced there was a guest in our bedchamber. "How is that possible?" I asked. "We've been in the sitting room since we awoke, and except for you, no one has passed through here."

"I suspect she climbed in through the window."

"She? It's a woman?

"Actually, a young girl."

"Well, bring her here," I said.

The young girl appeared to be a teenager. She might have been attractive, but it was difficult to tell, since she was muddy, unkempt, and dressed in rags. She also appeared frightened.

"Who are you?" asked Lisa, "and what were you doing in our room?"

The girl did not answer but stood there looking down, staring at her bare and grimy feet.

"Do you speak our language?" asked Lisa. "I asked who are you?"

There was a long pause before she answered, "I am nobody."

"What are you talking about? Everyone is somebody. Do you have a name?"

She remained silent a while longer, and then said, "My name is Elissa, which means wanderer, but I am also called Tyro, because I am a beginner who knows very little."

"Which name do you prefer?"

"My real name is Elissa. The other name was given to me by my master."

"Your master? Are you a slave?"

"Yes, but I shall not remain a slave. I am running away to become free."

"Why are you telling us that? Don't you realize that if others found out you could be severely punished? My God, you're in terrible trouble."

"I don't care. I'm tired of running, and if I cannot become a free person, I don't care what happens to me."

Lisa asked, "When did you last eat?"

"Two days ago I stole some figs from the marketplace."

"Sit down and have something to eat." Elissa sat and had some cheese and fruit. She ate slowly, but the way she relished each bite made it obvious she had suffered considerable hunger.

"Why are you running away?" I asked. "Does your master treat you badly?"

"Sometimes. But my master intends to sell me, and I fear a new master will treat me worse."

"But you don't really know that. How did you become a slave?" I asked.

"My family owns a small farm in Eleusis, and two years ago they were deeply in debt. The only things of value they had, besides the farm, were their children. My parents kept my two brothers, because they were needed to work on the farm, but I was considered unnecessary, so they sold me to the man who became my master."

What a horrible thing to do to a child, I thought. No one deserves that fate. I was reminded of *Uncle Tom's Cabin*, the groundbreaking anti-slavery novel written just before the Civil War. It was a story that changed forever how Americans viewed slavery. As the book opens a slave owner is forced to sell two slaves in order to satisfy his debt—exactly like Elissa's parents. One of the slaves is Uncle Tom, and the other is the son of Eliza, a central character. When Eliza hears her master's plan she runs away with her son and heads north to be free. Eliza, like our uninvited guest, Elissa, believes that a new master portends an ominous future. I found the similarities between the novel and the real life situation disturbing. The fictitious Eliza survives and becomes free, but Uncle Tom's new master, Simon Legree, is so abusive, Uncle Tom eventually dies. The fate of Elissa was still unknown, but it did not look promising.

First things first, I thought. I called Thea and told her to give our young guest a bath and provide her with some clean clothes. Then I sought out Zoe to discuss the situation. The matter of runaway slaves was completely beyond me; I needed expert advice.

"Slaves are generally treated well," Zoe said. "Much better than in Sparta, for example. They suffer little social prejudice and often appear the same as free men. That is why one is forbidden to strike a slave, because you might be striking a free man and not even know it. Slaves have considerable freedom; however, they don't have the same rights as citizens, and so they may not vote. But, of course, women are not permitted to vote either.

Runaways are a different story. They are treated harshly, as you can appreciate. If every slave in Athens suddenly decided to run away there would be social chaos. Slaves are treated well so that most don't feel the need to rebel or escape. But the penalty for those who do run away is often a flogging or sometimes being branded on their foreheads. They do this so they will forever be recognized as rebels. If, however, your visitor was mistreated, she may gain the right of sanctuary in a temple and appeal to the authorities to be sold to another master. That is her choice."

"But being sold to another master is precisely the reason she ran away."

"I will speak to her," said Zoe, "but I am not optimistic about her future."

Elissa suddenly appeared, and for a moment, I did not recognize her. Thea had washed and arranged her long hair in a most attractive way. She wore a short white tunic, new sandals, and her blue eyes almost glowed. She was stunning. The very thought of a hot iron branding that unblemished forehead seemed barbaric in the extreme.

I began to wonder about the Greek concept of slavery. I suppose it was little different from other slave societies, but since slavery was abolished in the U.S. a hundred and fifty years earlier, we rarely thought about the conditions that now surrounded us. I wondered why it was ever legal for anyone to dehumanize another. How could a person own another person in the same way he owned a goat or a donkey or a straw hat? These were concepts I found alien and repulsive. I decided to visit Socrates to get his judicious views on the subject.

"Slavery," Socrates began, "is an indisputable fact of life. It is the system that unifies the strength and greatness of our society. As men rule naturally over women, so too, are some men natural rulers while other men are natural slaves.

"With all due respect, Socrates, your logic is flimsier than a two-legged stool. Permit me to argue the other side of your reasoning. First of all, slavery may be a fact of life in Greece, but it is not a fact of life in other parts of the world, including where I come from. And to suggest that Greek society would not have achieved its greatness without slavery is simply a convenient opinion, not a provable fact. Finally, there is nothing *natural* about the status of women, freemen, or even slaves. All people are created equal, and their ultimate situation in life is a matter of circumstance. Slaves are not created by nature; they are created by the opportunity of one person to subjugate another.

"Your arguments have merit, George, but you overlook an important issue. True servitude is not a matter of status; it is a matter of spirit. Freedom of spirit is all that matters. A slave must strive to be the master of himself. If he can achieve that he will no longer be a slave."

"When one is so hopelessly wrong, we often say he is full of beans. Beans, as you know, produce gas, and gas is pretty much hot air. In other words, your argument is fallacious. Slavery is not a state of mind, as you suggest; it is a state of being totally dominated by another. You have famously said that virtue is the most valuable of all possessions. Since virtue is the quality of being morally good, how can you believe that slavery is morally good? It is precisely the opposite; it is morally reprehensible. Even your great playwright, Euripides has said, *Slavery, that thing of evil, is by its nature evil.* The problem, as I see it, is that never having been a slave, you know nothing about living a life totally devoid of freedom—a life where others make every choice for you. I am afraid we will not agree on this subject, but I can tell you this with absolute certainty: There will come a time when slavery in this world is abolished, and many will wonder how this shameful condition was allowed to exist for so long."

"It is possible you are right, George, but I doubt that it will happen in my lifetime. But now tell me, how have you and Lisa been getting along? When we were last together there were some unresolved difficulties between you two. For one of the problems I suggested a diet of walnuts. So, since we were last together, what has been going on?"

"We made love once since we last met. It was an odd experience arranged by Aphrodite. Neither of us knew that our partner was also our spouse. It was, however, an incredible sexual encounter, which proved to us both that there remains something extraordinary between us. As for the walnuts, I really can't say. But if Lisa becomes pregnant as a result of your advice, I guarantee we will name the child in your honor."

Socrates laughed and said, "That is unnecessary, but I am flattered by the thought."

I visited Socrates again the following day, and I brought along the slave girl, Elissa. This was to be an experiment of sorts, but no one, other than I, knew that. I spoke to Elissa the evening before and was amazed by her mature intellect and ability to express rational opinions. For someone so young she was extremely bright and personable. I warned her to speak up clearly, as Socrates had a hearing problem.

"I'd like you to meet a new friend of mine, Socrates. Her name is Elissa. She comes from Eleusis, and we met just two days ago. She is wise for her young age and has a unique philosophy of life that I thought you would appreciate."

"I am pleased to meet you, Elissa. Any friend of George is a friend of mine."

"Thank you, sir. I have heard much about your views on morality, virtue, and how one should properly conduct one's life, and I am honored to meet you."

"With regard to our discussion about slavery yesterday," I began, "my new friend has a unique perspective."

"How so?" asked Socrates.

"I have seen it first hand and up close," said Elissa, "and I feel strongly about the subject. You have said that some people are natural slaves. How would you say that manifests itself?"

"If you view a slave," said Socrates, "you will notice that he stands a certain way, holds his head at a certain angle, and responds to his master's orders in a compliant and submissive way. These mannerisms define the appearance of your typical slave."

"Would you say those traits are the natural habit of that person, or is it the result of being a slave and wishing to avoid punishment? In other words, what part does fear play in what you perceive as one's natural state?"

"An interesting question, Elissa. I sense you do not entirely agree with my observations."

"I greatly respect your opinion, sir, but you do not seem to recognize that a slave acts differently from a freeman simply because he *is* a slave, and not because he was born with any so-called natural tendencies. If, in fact, you were a slave I suspect you would be more compliant and submissive in you dealings with others than you now appear to be."

"You have apparently given this issue a great deal of thought," said Socrates. "Why does this subject interest someone as young as you?"

"Because," said Elissa, "I have been a slave for two miserable years, and I am currently a runaway who wishes to remain free. Freedom is something you take for granted, but it is something I have been denied for a very long time."

Socrates appeared genuinely shocked and remained silent for a while. Finally he said, "I am truly sorry for your situation, and I am astonished at your admission. You are unlike any slave I have ever met, and I realize I may have grossly underestimated your predicament."

"I would only wish that you remember this, sir: no rational person has ever voluntarily renounced his dignity and respect to become a slave."

"I shall remember that, Elissa, and let me say that our meeting today has been quite a revelation. I want to thank you and George for enlightening me on this subject."

While walking back to the inn I complemented Elissa on the intelligence and logic of her presentation. "You were terrific, and I think you may have convinced Socrates to give more thought to his rigid ideas about slavery."

"I'm pleased about that," she said, "but now what about my problem?"

"I think I have that figured out," I said.

On the following day I met with Elissa's master, Lygrisse, who had arrived at the inn to reclaim his runaway slave. Lygrisse appeared coarse and belligerent. He wore a hostile expression as we shook hands, as though he suspected I had something to do with Elissa's escape.

I learned earlier that the slave owner was deeply in debt, so I said, "If you would consider selling your slave, I believe I can remedy your problem. What is her value?"

"I am four hundred drachmas in debt," he answered. "I would consider an offer that is at least half that amount."

"My offer will exceed that amount by at least fourfold," I said, "since I propose to trade for your slave a rare device you have never seen before; a device so wondrous there is not another like it in all of Greece. This amazing apparatus is an electric toothbrush. It was devised to clean teeth, but it does more than that—much more. It is an amulet that provides protection against disease, pain, and misfortune—*all in your mouth* was the part I left out. If you choose to sell this incredible device you should receive at least twice the amount of your debt."

"How does it work?" asked Lygrisse.

I presented the device and said, "Push this button and hold tight."

He did as I suggested. The tip of the toothbrush began to spin wildly, and Lygrisse's faint smile quickly turned into a giggle. Then the giggle became unrestrained, rollicking laughter.

"Settle down," I said. "Now put it against your teeth".

"Amazing!" cried Lygrisse. "It is a miracle! I'm not sure I can part with it."

Lygrisse was completely hooked; he believed the electric toothbrush possessed magical powers, and, in fact, it did. It would keep him free of cavities for a few weeks, or at least until the battery needed recharging. By that time I hoped to be back in the twenty-first century.

I next spoke to Zoe and convinced her to hire Elissa as an executive assistant to help run the inn. It seemed the perfect position for a bright young girl, and it would relieve Zoe of much responsibility for her growing business. In other words, it was a winning solution for all.

Elissa hugged me, and through her tears expressed her gratitude for buying her freedom. Zoe also hugged me and thanked me for solving a multitude of problems with one deft move. I began to feel like Santa Claus on Christmas morning. The only downside, if you could even call it that, was using my old, conventional toothbrush from now on; but it seemed a small price to pay.

When we retired to our room Lisa gave me a hug and a huge kiss. "You did a wonderful thing today, George, and I love you for it."

"I have to agree; it worked our better than I dared hoped. Amazingly, everybody's happy."

"Move a little closer, I want to express my admiration for your brilliance."

"Why Lisa, this is so sudden."

"Oh, be quiet and kiss me."

THIRTEEN

Early the following morning I found Elissa in the courtyard. "I never asked you," I began, "if you really wanted to work for Zoe. I just assumed it would be a good idea for you both. But now that you're a free person, you have choices. You can remain here, find work elsewhere, or return to your family's farm in Eleusis."

"What you planned and what came to pass was the ideal solution for me. I liked Zoe the moment we met, and having the opportunity to work for her brings me more happiness than I have had in years. Returning to my family, on the other hand, is not at all an option. I can never forget they sold me into slavery. They thought only of their money problems. They thought little of my welfare, less of my happiness, and nothing at all of my future. I will never forgive them for their lack of concern, and I will never, ever, return to Eleusis."

"That is your choice; but still, they are your family."

"No," she said with tears in her eyes, "my family ceased to exist when they abandoned me to a slave owner." I could see that Elissa had determined her future, and her family would not be a part of it.

Later that morning I saw Aphrodite, and I asked a question that had been on my mind for several days. "Since Lisa and I are getting along pretty well these days, we'd like to return home. Obviously we need your help, so when do you think that could happen?"

"You do seem to be doing well, George. In fact, there is the unmistakable glow of sexual satisfaction about you this morning."

"I must say you're perceptive and awfully good at what you do."

"Of course; every goddess is the best at what she does. However, I had hoped you would become the loving couple you once were. I don't think you're quite there yet."

"You must know," I said, "the initial passion of a relationship fades with time. One cannot sustain a sky-high level of intensity forever; otherwise, one would never do anything more than make love day and night forever. That might be an appropriate life-style for you, the goddess of love; but mere mortals must get out of bed every so often to deal with more mundane matters—like making a living."

"I understand what you are saying, but let me think about that. By the way," she continued, "before leaving Athens, is there anything you wish to do, or perhaps someone you'd like to meet?"

I considered that for a moment and then answered, "As a matter of fact, I've greatly admired two of your heroic mortals for many years. The first is Pythagoras, the mathematician and philosopher, and the other is Aesop, who wrote fables. Would it be possible to meet them?"

"Not very likely, since both died many years ago. But I will think about that as well."

Aphrodite returned the following day with surprising answers to my questions.

"I thought about what you said yesterday," she began, "and you have a point. Remaining here may have diminishing benefits. You both know what you must do to improve your relationship, and I trust you can do that at home, as well as here. If you keep in mind all you have learned and experienced you may eventually attain the love your relationship has lacked. Now about visiting Pythagoras and Aesop, there is a way to do that, but it comes with great risk. You must enter the underworld, where they both reside, and though that is not an easy matter, returning to the world of the living is an even greater problem. Mortals have been known to visit the underworld and return to earth, all in one piece, but it is extremely rare."

I found the notion of visiting the underworld bizarre in the extreme. It was at least as implausible as visiting dead relatives in heaven. How many people, other than those hallucinating during a séance, had ever done that? And even if it could be done, how would I present this to Lisa? Even in my own rational mind the idea sounded nuttier than a fruitcake. But wasn't our very existence in ancient Greece just as preposterous?

"When you say a visit to the underworld comes with great risk, are you talking about issues of life and death?"

"Quite possibly," she replied. "Hades, the god who rules that realm, forbids anyone who enters the underworld to return to the region of light. A few have famously escaped, but each was a special case. You may have heard of Orpheus and Eurydice."

"I am familiar with that myth."

"It is no myth; it actually happened. I was there. Who dares to say otherwise?"

"I was only referring to *Bullfinch's Mythology*, a book that contains many early Greek events. I would guess he called the book "mythology" because he believed most of the stories were fables. If you two ever met, however, I'm sure he would change his mind."

"As you know, Orpheus returned from the underworld unharmed, though he lost Eurydice because he violated Persephone's instructions."

"Yes, I remember. He looked back, and Eurydice was suddenly gone—returned to the underworld forever."

"Hercules was another example of someone who outwitted Hades. His final labor was to capture Cerberus, Hades' three-headed dog. He succeeded, but only because he was guided by Hermes and protected by Athena. Without their help, the outcome would likely have been different. The same is true of Aeneas, Theseus, and Sisyphus; all were exceptional cases. You must not assume you would have the same good fortune."

That afternoon I reluctantly spoke to Lisa about a visit to the underworld. I knew she would find the idea bizarre, but I was totally unprepared for the eruption my idea precipitated. It was like the bad old Lisa on steroids. She sat quietly for the first few moments, as I described the proposed visit to the underworld. Then her entire being transmuted into a fire-spitting virago.

"Have you completely lost your mind? You want to visit the underworld? Have you any idea what goes on down there? The place is filled with dead people! Totally dead people! It's like touring a cemetery six feet below ground. Is this some extreme form of gallows humor? Honest to God, I don't understand you."

"Take it easy, it was only an idea."

"A preposterous and grotesque idea, if you don't mind my saying. You are demented, George—totally over the edge! Of all the insane ideas you've ever had this one takes the cake! If you insist on going, go right ahead. Have a wonderful trip, but don't bother to drop a card."

"Calm down, Lisa. I only thought a visit with two historic geniuses would be an incredible experience—something we would remember for the rest of our lives."

"Provided there would *be* a rest of our lives. What if we wound up as permanent residents? What then? Is your incredible experience worth dying for?"

"I would never propose an idea if I believed it would fail."

"But you have no assurance it will succeed."

"Just keep an open mind, and I'll investigate the idea further. If it looks to be too dangerous I'll drop the whole thing. But let's not have this come between us."

"Too late! It's already come between us. This is so unbelievably insane, so totally off the wall, I'm not even sure you're the same man I married."

I could see that our partially repaired relationship was still fragile; and if there were a showdown between the underworld and our marriage, I was prepared to ditch the underworld.

As I reviewed the stories of those who successfully returned from the underworld it became clear that one had to enlist the help of a powerful deity in order to succeed. Going up against Hades on one's own would be suicidal. The obvious answer for us, of course, was Aphrodite, but because of a long-standing feud between her and Persephone, Hades wife and goddess of the underworld, she was not entirely welcome in their realm. The two had competed for the love of Adonis years before, and the dispute required Zeus to decree that the handsome god would split his time between the two goddesses. Though all that was long ago, ill will remained between the two.

"Do you think you could convince Persephone to help us?" I asked Aphrodite.

"Our relationship is not the best," she replied, "but she still owes me a few favors. Let me speak to her, and perhaps we can find a way to make this work."

Two days later Aphrodite appeared and said, "What luck! Persephone is having her usual marital problems, and she sees your visit as a way to frustrate her obstinate husband. She greeted me amiably and even thanked me for the opportunity this presents. You know, there has always been friction between those two. She did not submit to Hades willingly, but was abducted by him while picking flowers one day. A woman does not forget such trickery and violence; and though it was long ago, she remains resentful. She has agreed to help and guarantees your safe return to the world of the living."

"But can we trust her? There is much at risk here."

"I am confident we can, since she will gain personally from this venture."

"So, how would this work?"

"Your old friend Hermes is the official escort for the dead to the afterlife. He is the only deity, other than Hades and Persephone, who may freely enter and leave the underworld. Hermes would take you directly to Elysium, which is a section of the underworld in which reside those souls considered heroic and virtuous. It is there you will find Pythagoras and Aesop, who are forever blessed and continue to enjoy a happy existence. When your visit concludes, Persephone herself will guide you out of the underworld and back to where your adventure began."

"So, what could possibly go wrong?" I asked. "It all sounds too easy."

"There are no absolute guarantees," she answered, "but your visit should be relatively free of problems. I suppose Hades could discover your presence, and that might create some danger. But Persephone assures me he will be in no position to interfere. She proposes to give him a potion that will keep him unconscious for several hours. By the time he wakes, you will be gone and she will then have the pleasure of taunting him with the story of your inappropriate visit."

"This is beginning to sound like a soap opera."

"A soap opera; what is that?"

"It's a melodrama with a lot of emotion and excitement."

"Well, let's hope your visit will be more serene."

My next task was to convince Lisa that our proposed visit to the underworld would be as safe as a walk in the park, since the goddess of the underworld herself would be our sponsor. Hermes would lead us in, and Persephone would guarantee our safe return. How could she possibly object to that arrangement?

"Are you crazy? You trust Hermes to lead us there? The same Hermes who kidnapped me and came within a pubic hair of attempted rape? And what do you really know about Persephone? How do you know she'll keep her word? And if she doesn't, what do we do, sue her? This plan of yours sounds more idiotic than ever. Is it really worth a death-defying effort to schmooze with a couple of dead Greeks?"

"You're being negative, Lisa; this is the opportunity of a lifetime."

"The last time I heard that line we ended up owning an empty patch of sand in the Mojave Desert. This time it could literally be the end of us. No thanks!"

She needs more time, I thought. Once she thinks it over and realizes this is an incredible adventure, she'll change her mind. She loves excitement; she thrives on melodrama; given enough time she'll see this as an extraordinary opportunity. Unless, of course, I'm completely wrong.

Lisa held out for another day. "I don't want to hear another word about your trip to the underworld. I believe it's foolish and reckless, and I think you're obsessed and deranged." But the following day she spoke to Aphrodite. I have no idea what was said, but suddenly there was a crack in her armor. "Tell me again," she began, "what do you know about Pythagoras and Aesop?"

"Well, Pythagoras was a brilliant philosopher who actually coined that term. It means one who loves wisdom. You may remember hearing his name in beginning geometry. The Pythagorean theorem, which applies to right-angled triangles, is what he is best known for today. But essentially he was a talented and rather eccentric genius who dabbled in math, music, and mysticism. Some believe he was a blend of brilliance and madness."

"Like most geniuses, I suppose," said Lisa.

"He also left us hundreds of insightful proverbs." For example, *Choose always the way that seems best, however rough it may be.*"

"Was that meant for me?" asked Lisa.

"He also said, *Let no one persuade you to do or say whatever is not best for you.*"

"I'm beginning to like this guy," she said. "Tell me more."

"*The shortest words, yes and no, are those which require the most thought.*"

"Okay, I'm giving your proposal the most thought. Now, what about Aesop?"

"I discovered Aesop when I was about twelve years old. I thought his fables were imaginative and entertaining, and the morals of his stories read like something out of Benjamin Franklin's *Poor Richard's Almanac.* Aesop said: *Look before you leap*, and *Necessity is the mother of invention*, whereas Franklin said: *Honesty is the best policy.* Those could have been written by the same person, don't you agree?"

"They all sound pretty hackneyed today."

"Perhaps, but they are eternal truths. How can you argue with: *Those who seek to please everybody please nobody*, or: *You cannot escape your fate*? And you have to appreciate the way that Aesop presented his fables. Almost all involved talking creatures that were featured in dramatic incidents before the fable ended with the moral of the story. For example, you've probably heard one of his most famous stories about the Hare and the Tortoise."

The Hare was boasting of his speed before the other animals. He claimed to never have been beaten and then proposed to race anyone at all. None but the Tortoise accepted his challenge. The Hare began to laugh and proclaimed he would dance circles around him all the way. As the race began the Hare darted nearly out of sight, but soon stopped. To show contempt for the Tortoise, he lay down and took a nap. The Tortoise plodded on, and when the Hare awoke, he saw the Tortoise cross the finish line.

Moral of the story: *Slow but steady wins the race.*

"You've convinced me," said Lisa. These guys sound charming—I'd love to meet them."

"Great!" I said. But now I began to worry; would this adventure go off as smoothly as I hoped, or would one of a million conceivable things go wrong?

FOURTEEN

I was up half the night worrying about our trip to the realm of Hades and imagining the dangers we might face. The list of potential problems was endless, but if I concentrated on them, chances are I'd never get out of bed. I finally fell asleep at about three in the morning and dreamed we were in the underworld. It was a dark and dismal place, and the air was as cold and clammy as Carlsbad Cavern. The place looked like a stage set from every zombie movie I'd ever seen. Dead people in tattered rags were in constant motion, shuffling along, ostensibly going nowhere. They looked straight ahead and seemed to be mumbling, but the sounds were unintelligible. At one point a gaunt figure approached, and I noticed his eyes were black, empty sockets. He raised an arm, as if to touch me, and I swatted away his bony hand. I was overcome by panic and began to run, but run where? I was lost and confused and had no idea which way to go. My heart began to beat faster as I realized there *was* no escape. I had never been more terrified in my life.

Then I heard Lisa say, "How beautiful!"

I was suddenly awake and Lisa was standing in the doorway watching the warm sun rise above the horizon. In response to my groan she asked, "Are you okay?"

"I think so. I just had a terrible dream, but I'll be fine."

"You're not worried about the underworld, are you?" Was it *that* obvious, I wondered?

"Are you kidding? What's there to worry about?"

"I don't know, but you look awfully pale."

"Just wait 'til I have my walnuts; I'll be ready to conquer the world. You'll see."

Aphrodite arrived late in the morning and asked if we were ready for our big adventure. "Wear something warm," she advised. "It's cool down there."

"Doesn't sound like our kind of hell," commented Lisa.

"There is no heaven or hell," I said. "It's one big graveyard for good and for bad."

Hermes appeared shortly after Aphrodite's arrival, and it was an awkward reunion. During our last encounter Hermes had delivered Lisa back home and was quickly on his way. I had successfully frightened him by describing the dangers she posed as a potential sexual partner, and he had fallen for every terrifying fantasy I created. Now the reformed rapist stood some distance from Lisa and was deferential in his behavior.

"Nice to see you both," he said uncomfortably. "I hope you are well."

"Now that I'm back where I belong," said Lisa, "I am quite well."

"I apologize again," he said, "for our previous misunderstanding." Hermes characterized his abduction of Lisa as a "misunderstanding", but to Lisa it was a kidnapping and attempted rape.

"All that is past," I said, "and now we are off on a new adventure."

"Yes," said Hermes, "it is my responsibility to escort you to the underworld. I am happy for your sake that it is only a visit and not your final trip there. Shall we begin?"

We said our goodbyes to Zoe and her staff, and I dared wonder if we would ever see them again. We walked for nearly an hour, and finally came upon a clearing outside the city that was heavily wooded with poplars and willow trees. Who could guess that access to the land of the dead would have such a lovely and peaceful entrance? The landscape reminded me of Forest Lawn. We had been following the Acheron River, known as the River of Woe, and suddenly the stream narrowed and began its swift descent into the large opening below ground.

"This is where we begin our descent into Hades' kingdom," announced Hermes. We followed the watercourse as it dropped further and then widened again to a sizable river. We were now completely below the surface of the earth, and as the light began to fade we felt currents of cool and damp air. There was an odd aroma I could not immediately identify, but I eventually assumed it was the faint smell of decay. It was the most sinister place I'd ever been, but Lisa oddly commented, "Isn't this exciting?" And to think I had to talk her into this adventure.

After another twenty minutes we arrived at an intersecting river called the Styx. It was one of the many rivers that converged at the center of the underworld. We were forced to cross this river to reach the entrance to Hades' realm. A single ferryboat was available for that purpose, and the ferryman was Charon, who had held this post for many years. Originally an Athenian seaman, Charon was now a full time ferryman whose responsibility was to take dead souls across the river to their final resting place. He charged a small fee for this service consisting of a coin generally placed in the dead person's mouth. From living persons he demanded a golden bough that was obtained from the Cumaean Sibyl. Who dreamed up *that* one? Fortunately, Hermes remembered to bring the bough.

Charon was a typical seaman—a bit scruffy, with a crooked nose and rough, unkempt beard. He was known to be cantankerous and generally unpleasant; but considering his job, who wouldn't be? He wore a loincloth, an odd, conical hat, and in his right hand was a well-worn ferryman's pole. Hermes offered the ferryman the golden bough, and we stepped aboard the shallow boat.

According to myth, three brothers, Zeus, Poseidon, and Hades, defeated the Titans and claimed sovereignty of the cosmos. Zeus ended up ruling the air; Poseidon, the sea; and Hades, the underworld. The earth was available to all three, and each had equal access to Mount Olympus. Though Hades became the wealthiest, because he claimed the valuable ores within the earth, he was also the most feared and reviled, since he was intimately associated with death.

Our trip took fewer than ten minutes, during which it seemed we passed from one world into another, which in fact, we had. When we reached the adamantine gate, Charon exclaimed—with little subtlety—"Everybody off the boat!" We had arrived at the entrance to the underworld. The adamantine gate derived from "adamant", meaning unyielding, which I suppose informed a corpse this was truly the end of the line. Cerberus, the mythical three-headed dog, guarded the gate; but at the moment he looked anything but mythical. He appeared quite real and ferocious enough to tear you apart three times faster than a pit bull.

"Nice Cerberus," said Hermes petting the furry middle head. "You remember me, don't you? These people are friends, so please behave and let's not make trouble."

I could not believe he was reasoning with this terrifying creature. Nevertheless, the large beast backed away, and we passed through the gate. I was told that Cerberus occasionally allowed people to enter the underworld, but he never, ever, permitted anyone to leave. Our exit would be Persephone's responsibility, but I didn't dare think about that now.

We were officially in the realm of the dead, and it looked like every horror movie I'd ever seen. Shadows of dead souls surrounded us, and filmy images floated through the air.

"It reminds me of the Haunted House at Disneyland," said Lisa.

"Except this is for real. These floating things were actually people."

"Still," she said, "it's exciting, and not as scary as the Disney version." So far, so good, I thought. Wait until Hades discovers we're here and the fireworks begin.

"We are now heading to the Elysian Fields," said Hermes, "where reside the distinguished people you wish to see. It is not more than another fifteen minutes from here."

We had put our complete trust in Hermes, and I realized he could have told us anything. We were traveling through a labyrinthine landscape consisting of deformed trees, coarse shrubbery, and rock-strewn hills. It was impossible to know exactly where we were. I recalled my first trip to Venice, during which I was constantly lost. I recognized the famous St. Marks Square, but set me down a block away and I could have been anywhere else in Italy. That's how the underworld appeared to me—totally bewildering. To make matters worse, the entire region was sunless and unpleasant. It was a joyless place, a hopeless place, and—not surprisingly—a place most avoided as long as they possibly could.

Lisa summed it up neatly when she said, "It's a bit depressing, don't you think?"

"A bit?" I asked. "The underworld is the largest graveyard that's ever been; there is nothing here but death! How could *anything* be more depressing?"

"Just ahead are the Elysian Fields," said Hermes. "This is where I leave you. Persephone should be along in a while to lead you back to the world of the living."

"Can you hang around until she gets here?" asked Lisa. "Without you, we're totally lost."

"You'll be fine. Persephone will definitely be here; she is quite reliable." And with that he turned and walked back along the path we had just traveled. We were now alone; alone in the bowels of the underworld, and my anxiety level surged like a rocket leaving the launching pad.

"Nothing to worry about," I bravely said, but I was literally whistling past the graveyard.

"Are you sure?" asked Lisa.

"Of course I'm sure. Let's carry on and do what we came to do."

The Elysian Fields were like the Garden of Eden compared to the area through which we just hiked. It was beautifully landscaped and reminiscent of a posh country club. This special area of the underworld was available to heroes and other distinguished souls. We noticed people wandering about, talking, debating, and playing games. What a great life, I thought, until I suddenly realized: there *was* no life; there was nothing here but death.

"Excuse me," I said to a group near the entrance, "where might I find Pythagoras?"

"Do you mean Pythagoras the vegetarian?" asked an older man.

"I was thinking more of Pythagoras the philosopher."

"Everyone here is a philosopher."

"But this Pythagoras is also a mathematician."

"Oh, you must mean Pythagoras, the oddest of odd ducks. Come with me." The old man led the way, and after a few minutes we stopped at the shore of a placid lake. Sitting alone on a stone bench beneath a tree was a man throwing pebbles into the water. The man appeared fairly old, and his handsome, narrow face sported a well-trimmed gray beard.

"Excuse me, sir," said our guide, "are you Pythagoras?"

"Indeed I am," answered the man. "What can I do for you?"

"This gentleman here was looking for you—and now you've been found."

"Hello," I said. "My name is George, and this is my wife, Lisa."

"Pleased to make your acquaintance," he said with a pleasant smile.

"We hope we're not disturbing you, but we've come a long way to speak with you. By the way, why were you throwing pebbles into the lake?"

"It may have appeared a meaningless pastime induced by boredom, but I can assure you it had a serious purpose. I was studying the concentric rings that rippled outward from where the pebbles hit the water. These I believe represent energy that transfers the force of the impact away from the initial point at which the pebble enters the lake."

"I don't quite understand, said Lisa"

"I think I do," I said. "It's similar to the sudden release of energy resulting from an earthquake. Seismic waves radiate outward from the epicenter."

"Are you an engineer?" asked Pythagoras.

"I'm an architect, and we come from an area that has experienced many earthquakes."

"As you may know, Poseidon causes such phenomena. He is the god of earthquakes."

"Well, we have a slightly different explanation; but what the hell, let's blame Poseidon. You may not know it, but you have become quite famous for your geometric theorem regarding the proportion of right triangles. Believe it or not, thousands of years from now every schoolchild will be familiar with the Pythagorean theorem. How do you feel about that?"

"If that is true it is flattering, but I would prefer to be known as a philosopher. I have said that the basis for everything, including the divine principles of the universe, can be expressed in terms of their relationships to numbers."

"Do you really mean *everything*?"

"Indeed I do; including the visual arts, music, and poetry. They all can be best understood through the study of mathematics."

"I once read that you believed the earth was a sphere in the center of the universe. Is that really what you said?"

"Yes, and for that I was severely criticized. But I still believe the earth is spherical, because a sphere is the most perfect solid figure. To me, that is a reasonable proposition."

"Well, you were centuries ahead of your time, but let me assure you, you were correct.

Now, let me ask about your private life. Little is known, but everyone seems to have a theory about whether you were married or had children or even the way you died. Can you clear that up?

"I was not married, but I lived for many years with one of my disciples. Her name was Theano, and we had two children, both girls. Theano was charming, bright, and an excellent mathematician. Unfortunately she died in childbirth when she was still quite young."

"That must have been a great tragedy for you," said Lisa.

"It was, and it remains so. About my death, that is another sad story. A powerful man by the name of Cylon applied to become a disciple in my society. After some consideration I rejected him because of his questionable character. He was abrasive, dishonest, and was known to have bouts of violence—not at all the sort of individual we wanted in our society. Two weeks later Cylon's henchmen, seeking vengeance, attacked me one night, and I died of my wounds the following day. I was, as you see me, an old man, but I fully intended to live several more years."

"That is a very unhappy story," I said. "Can you tell us more about your society?"

"My society was based on the principles of what I believe to be just and reasonable. For example, we believed men and women should be treated equally and that all property should be held in common. Neither of these concepts was very popular at that time. As vegetarians we considered eating meat an abomination, and we also believed it was sinful to eat beans."

"Hold on," I said. "I understand equality for sexes, even vegetarianism, but beans? Why is it a sin to eat beans? And do you mean all beans, even garbanzos?" Pythagoras began to blush, but he remained silent. Later, as I thought about it, I suspected he was embarrassed by flatulence, which is often caused by beans. After all, fellow corpses defined him as the oddest of odd ducks.

"Are you aware," I asked, "that many of your contemporaries consider you an inseparable blend of genius and—how can I put this delicately—somewhat unbalanced, a bit loony, actually?"

"I believe one must be satisfied with doing good, and leave others to speak of you as they please. I also think making enemies is unwise, so I ignore what is said about me and avoid arguments. How I am defined by others is really of little interest."

"You seem content in your beliefs," said Lisa, "but doesn't criticism bother you?"

"Most criticism, I find, has little more value than silence," he replied.

"I understand you don't have much respect for theology," I said, "and only slight regard for the gods. What then do you consider your faith?"

"I believe the mystery of the divine can be found in common sense rational thought. That is my abiding faith, and truly, I believe it is all anyone should need. I am aware that many disagree with me; they insist that gods control the vicissitudes of life. But that, I believe, is a convenient excuse for abdicating personal responsibility. When faced with a difficult decision it is always easier to step aside, believing the answer is in the hands of the gods. And by so doing one may remain blameless, regardless of how the matter is resolved."

"One last question, Pythagoras, have you any thoughts on a successful marriage?"

"That is an interesting subject," he said, "with little agreement on what constitutes success. Spouses, I believe, should be as companions on a journey. They should aid each other on the road to a happier life." I doubt that anyone could argue with that.

When we saw his head nod and eyelids flutter we knew it was time for his nap and the signal for us to leave. We thanked Pythagoras and reluctantly said goodbye.

"It was nice speaking to you," he said. "I hope your future days will be pleasant."

As we walked away Lisa asked, "How can you not love this guy?"

"I agree; he was everything I expected—bright, thoughtful, and self assured. He was so much more than his famous theorem, which is how most know him."

We were now on our way to visit Aesop, who resided a short walk from the lake at which we found Pythagoras. I had read much about Aesop but found little agreement about the details of his life. Most believed he was born a slave and later won his freedom by entertaining people with creative fables. He was known to be profoundly ugly and was described by one writer as a turnip with teeth. But all agreed his fables were brilliant lessons on the fundamental principles of life. I was fascinated by this unusual poet and hoped to learn more about him.

"You will find Aesop under a pomegranate tree in a small grassy field," we were told. As we came upon that site I noticed a number of people standing around a dwarfish individual who appeared to be lecturing. This had to be him, I thought; the unflattering descriptions fitted him perfectly. He had a hunched back, potbelly, and was truly unattractive. As he finished his story, I said, "Forgive the interruption, but we've come a long way to meet you. Have you a moment to speak with us?"

"A moment?" he asked, "I have the better part of eternity." And then he laughed at his macabre joke. "What do you wish to speak about?"

"Your famous fables; they have been celebrated for thousands of years."

"But I've only been dead for a hundred and thirty years," he said.

"Well, we come from the future, so trust me—you are a giant literary star."

"That's a bit odd, but nice to know. By the way, who are you?"

"My name is George, and this is my wife, Lisa. We are visitors to the underworld."

"I thought it was impossible to visit here."

"Ours is a special case. May we talk about your stories? For example, I've wondered why your fables are personified by animals that speak, solve problems, and have human qualities?"

"You should know that I began life as a slave. After I gained my freedom I rose to a position of renown representing a number of royal patrons. As both slave and freeman I could not very well bite the hand that was feeding me, so I substituted animals in place of real persons to avoid conflict. For example, do you know my story about the Peacock and the Crane?

A Peacock spread his dazzling tail and mocked a Crane that was passing by. 'I am robed like a king in gold and all colors of the rainbow, while you are ashen and colorless.'

'True' replied the Crane, 'but I am able to soar to the heights of heaven and lift my voice to the stars, while you walk below among the dunghills of the earth.'

The moral*: Fine feathers do not make fine birds.*

Now imagine for a moment what would happen if I portrayed my patron, Croesus, the king of Lydia, in place of the Peacock. Do you think I would have escaped punishment?"

"How clever of you!" said Lisa.

"It was not so much cleverness as the instinct of self-preservation."

"I understand you have faced other such situations."

"Are you referring to the fig episode? I can explain that. It began when I was unjustly accused of stealing figs. Now, how can one possibly defend such a claim? It occurred to me that the only way was the way I chose. I forced myself to throw up, and no evidence of figs was discovered. Dramatic perhaps, but again, drama prompted by desperation."

"The story I was thinking about involved a magistrate." I said.

"Oh yes, that episode was a rather close call. A magistrate, with no provocation whatsoever, took a dislike to me. He stopped me one day and asked where I was going. I figured it was a trap, so I remained silent. He insisted I answer, so I said I didn't know. That so annoyed him he ordered me arrested. On the way to prison I said, 'You see, I told the truth. When you asked me where I was going I didn't know it would be to prison.' The magistrate was so amused he let me go free."

"That's a wonderful story," I said. "I can see why your fables are so popular; you are inventive and have a charming sense of humor."

"That was generally true most of my life," said Aesop, "but no amount of invention could save me in the end. Perhaps you know the story. I was on an ambassadorial mission to Delphi, whose citizens had a reputation for piety and wisdom. However, what I discovered through my dealings was a community of arrogant, avaricious, and immoral people. I delivered my opinion of them through a barely disguised fable, as follows:

129

A young mouse begged his mother to allow him a first look at the outside world. 'Don't stay long,' she said 'and be careful.' The mouse scurried back in a few minutes to describe the creatures he saw. 'The first had soft fur and yellow eyes, and she waved her tail in the friendliest way. The other was a monster with sharp beak and claws who screeched cock-a-doodle-do.' The mother explained, 'the first creature was a cat, who loves to eat young mice; and the other was a chicken, who eats only seeds and grain. You had better learn the difference.'

The moral: *Appearances can be deceiving.*

Well, the Delphians saw right through the story and were greatly offended by my observation that they were not what they appeared to be. I was charged with sacrilege and thrown into prison. The next day I was taken to court and, though innocent of any crime, I was condemned to die. A magistrate visited me the next morning suggesting that if I confessed my offense, the judge might be lenient.

'But I committed no crime,' I said. 'Your citizens, however, instead of showing piety and wisdom, show just the opposite. It is you who should apologize to me.' Then, realizing it might very well be my death warrant I told the following story to illustrate my point:

A fox caught in a trap escaped, but in so doing, lost his tail. Facing a life of shame and ridicule, he devised a plan to convince all the other foxes that being tailless was actually a great advantage. 'Just look,' he said, 'I no longer carry the weight of that bushy appendage, and it is far more attractive as well.' One of the foxes interrupted to ask, 'If you had not lost your tail, would you still counsel us this way?'

The moral: *Misery loves company.*

'You, sir,' I said, 'are the fox with no tail, and you wish to amputate my tail for no other reason than it will lessen the shame of your behavior.' The magistrate said, 'Your impudence and lack of remorse has proved the truth of your guilt.'

'But there are two side to all truths,' I replied. 'Sadly, that was my last gasp. Within the hour I was flung to my death from a great precipice into a rocky canyon below. So here I am in the underworld, a bit prematurely, as far as I'm concerned, but here forever, nonetheless."

"What an appalling story!" said Lisa. "How unjust and senseless!"

"Yes," said Aesop, "indeed it was. But eventually we all end up here, don't we?"

Listening to Aesop relate his stories had a strange affect. Here was one of the homeliest and misshapen of all men performing his creative tales. The illusion, however, was that the melodious voice and dramatic gestures belonged to an attractive and gifted performer. Reciting his fables transformed Aesop into another being—one that happened to be a profoundly talented entertainer.

As I was considering that thought, a strikingly beautiful woman suddenly appeared. "George, Lisa, I am Persephone. There is a problem, and you must come with me immediately! There is not a second to lose!"

I looked at Lisa; her face had turned completely white.

"Oh God," she said, "don't let this be what I think it is."

FIFTEEN

Years earlier, before she became Queen of the underworld, Persephone was a radiantly beautiful adolescent. She attracted the attention of many, including the powerful god Hades. She was not, however, his willing wife. Lacking the civility to woo her in the traditional way, Hades abducted her one morning while she was picking flowers in a field near her home. Suddenly the earth opened up, a chariot drawn by four black horses appeared, and the wily god of the underworld snatched Persephone away. He took her directly to his kingdom intending to make her his bride.

In protest of this wicked act Demeter, Persephone's mother and goddess of agriculture, cast a curse upon the land that caused a great famine. Zeus finally intervened and negotiated a compromise that permitted Persephone to return home. However, she was obliged to spend four months of each year in the underworld. Persephone actually grew to enjoy her role as Queen, even though it was intimately connected with Hades, whose presence continued to remind her of the abduction, rape, and forced marriage she suffered at his hands.

I learned most of these facts from *Bulfinch's Mythology*; and when Persephone suddenly appeared it was easy to understand Hades' obsession with her. She was truly stunning. But she seemed troubled as she repeated her message: "There is a problem."

"What kind of problem?" I asked.

"Hades suspects that non-dead outsiders have breached the underworld, and he is terribly distressed. That sort of thing drives the poor fool crazy."

"I thought he was unconscious, that you knocked him out."

"I prepared a potion, concealed it in his wine cup, and offered him a drink before dinner, as I normally do. Then the clumsy buffoon tripped over his own feet, fell over a chair, and spilled the entire contents. There was no opportunity to create a new potion."

"So he's awake and alert?"

"Awake and alert and convinced that something devious is going on."

"But what does he actually know?"

"Only that someone reported seeing you two speaking with Pythagoras."

"What can we do?" asked Lisa. No one had an answer until Aesop joined the conversation.

"First, you should avoid a remedy that is worse than the disease. Next, enthusiasm must not exceed discretion. Finally, never forget: The battle is not always won by the strong."

"With all due respect," said Persephone, "would you kindly shut up?"

"I was only trying to help," said the contrite fabulist.

"We don't need any more of your platitudes; we need a plan of action."

"Well, *excuse* me," said Aesop.

"Perhaps," I suggested, "we should hide somewhere until the crisis blows over. I'm sure by now every escape route is being watched."

"I suspect you're right," said Persephone. "But where do we hide you?" There was a long silence before she said, "It would have to be a place Hades would never think to look."

Then Aesop spoke up again. "The most obvious solutions are often in plain view."

"Well, thank you, old man," said Persephone. "You've just given me an idea. George, Lisa, I'm going to hide you in the very last place Hades would ever suspect. This is so delicious; if we pull this off, the pompous jackass will absolutely die of aggravation."

"What do you mean, *if* we pull this off?" asked Lisa. "Is there a chance we won't?"

"There are no guarantees," said Persephone, "but I'll do my best. Let's get going."

"Where?" I asked.

"Just follow me," said Persephone. "And trust me."

As we bid farewell to Aesop, he said, "Remember this, my friends: Wherever you are, there you will be." It made little sense and—sad to observe—indicated that the wise philosopher was becoming in death a sad caricature of himself. We set off with the Queen of the underworld, and though we had no idea what she had in mind, we were forced to trust her. After walking for half an hour, crossing two shallow streams and climbing a large hill, there appeared before us an immense structure. It was set in a lake and appeared as impressive as the Palace of Versailles.

"What in the world is this?" I asked.

"This is the House of Hades," answered Persephone. "It is the castle in which we live and the last place below earth that Hades will look for you."

The principal entrance was located at the end of a bridge that spanned a watery moat surrounding the palace. The entry door appeared about twenty feet high and was flanked by Ionic columns On the face of the door was the sculpted head of a monster with horns, fiery eyes, and a gaping mouth. It seemed that by simply passing through the front door one might be devoured. And if the sculpted monster didn't get you, the giant hound guarding the entrance certainly would. It was a fearful looking beast that was covered with matted black fur.

"What a ferocious looking dog!" said Lisa.

"He's not nearly as vicious as he appears," said Persephone. "His only function is to frighten away strangers. My husband dislikes most people and discourages unannounced visitors."

"He doesn't sound very sociable," I said.

"He's not; but then again, being sociable is by no means a major concern. I would characterize him as severe, and sadly, without a shred of humor. Of course, in the land of the dead not much *is* amusing."

We avoided the main entrance and circled the property towards the rear. At that point there was another bridge over the moat that led to a less pretentious entry that had neither guards nor vicious animals. As we crossed the bridge I asked Persephone if the moat was possibly stocked with piranhas or crocodiles.

"Of course not," she answered. "Do you think we're completely antisocial?" The thought had crossed my mind, but I decided to drop the subject. As we entered the fortress-like palace I wondered if Vlad Dracula had devised the depressing color scheme. It was black on black and gloomier than a graveyard in a rainstorm.

"This place could use a bit of color, don't you think?" asked Lisa.

"Well, if you had the job to reflect Hades' temperament wouldn't a dismal décor be the perfect expression?"

"I can't imagine having that kind of job," she answered.

Persephone led us down long corridors and through vast, empty halls, all of which were constructed of rough black stone. The polished marble floors were also as black as night. Torches spaced at regular intervals provided the only light. We eventually reached the Queen's Residence and were led through a large wooden door into a spacious reception area.

"These are my quarters," said Persephone. "Hades rarely visits here. When he needs to consult with me or requires that I fulfill my marital obligations he sends for me, and we meet in his quarters. Since he is seldom here I believe it is the perfect place for you to remain. It may be right under his nose, but you are safer here than any other place I can imagine."

"How about the help?" I asked. "I notice you have several slaves that attend to you."

"They are my personal property, and they are sworn to protect and defend me from all others, including Hades himself. They will never reveal your presence to anyone."

Persephone led us through another door to a private suite of spaces. "This will be your apartment for as long as you remain. There is a sitting room, bedchamber, and private bathroom. My chief slave, Kallista, will provide everything you may need. Her name means 'most beautiful', and I think you will agree she is."

Just then Kallista entered the room and her loveliness took my breath away. Her features were as exquisite as any fashion model's, and her figure seemed designed to drive men wild. She was absolutely dazzling, and I wondered how the Queen could employ someone who offered such serious competition for attention.

"May I bring you something to drink?" asked the beautiful slave. Her voice was as delightful as her appearance.

"That would be much appreciated," I answered.

"Watch your step, George," said Lisa.

"Take it easy; she only offered a drink, not a back rub."

"It often starts with a drink," Lisa said, "and . . .

"Oh please, you can't be serious. Here we are trapped in the underworld, surrounded by death, being hunted down by Hades himself, and you're concerned about me ogling a beautiful woman? Honestly, Lisa, don't we have enough to worry about?"

"I must leave you now," said Persephone. "Please make yourselves comfortable. I'll return later to discuss our next move. One way or another we will get you back to the world of the living."

"I hope we're still breathing when that happens," said Lisa. Persephone ignored the sarcasm and left without another word. Suddenly we were alone.

"What if she never returns?" asked Lisa. Strangely, I was thinking the very same thing.

"Of course she'll return. Do you think she wants us as permanent guests? She promised Aphrodite she'd get us out of here, and I believe some honor still exists among goddesses. I mean, if you can't trust a fellow goddess, who the hell *can* you trust?"

"Maybe you're right, but she and Aphrodite are hardly best friends. As a matter of fact, they're both still *shtupping* Adonis! How can there *not* be some antagonism there."

So there we were, in the House of Hades, being treated as guests but feeling more like prisoners. How on earth did we get into this mess? More importantly, how would we ever find our way back to the land of the living, or God forbid, the twenty-first century? And then suddenly, an incredible idea popped into my head. That's it, I thought. Why not? Why the hell not?

Persephone returned an hour later, by which time I had formulated an extraordinary plan.

"I have an idea to get us out of here, and I'd like to know what you think."

"Of course, George, I'm interested in hearing any plan that gets you back on earth safely."

"Do you remember how Hades abducted you many years ago?"

"I will never forget it."

"As I understand it, a chariot drawn by four black horses suddenly appeared while you were gathering flowers near your home. Hades drove through an opening in the earth's crust and whisked you away to the underworld. Am I right?"

"That's exactly what happened. And it was all done in the blink of an eye."

"Well, if Hades could do that, why couldn't we? What if we borrowed his chariot, found that opening, and did the very same thing? Can you think of any reason why it wouldn't work?"

"That is a marvelous idea, but there are risks involved—taking a chariot that's heavily guarded, finding the opening, and doing it all with great secrecy."

"Have you considered," interrupted my cynical wife, "that you don't know the first thing about driving a chariot? How do you propose managing four powerful stallions when your only experience with horses was an afternoon you spent at Santa Anita two years ago? Have you lost your mind?"

"How tough could it be to drive a chariot? If any old Athenian can drive a chariot, why not me? It couldn't be as complicated as driving an eighteen-wheel semi tractor-trailer."

"It's probably not as complicated as flying a jet fighter either, but as far as I know you've never done either of those things."

"You're missing the point. The chariot did it before, the horses already know their way. We'd just be passengers."

"I think I remember the location of the opening," said Persephone. "It's not far from here."

"Great!" I said. "Now we need is to find a way to 'borrow' the chariot."

"That's the problem," she said. "Hades keeps the chariot and horses well guarded and ready for use, in the event he has a sudden urge to travel. But I may have a plan of my own."

Persephone left, and we were alone again. I was enthused about my plan to escape the underworld, but Lisa still had doubts. She was seriously worried about the escape plan.

"I know you think swiping a chariot and driving to freedom is pretty wacky," I said, "but it seems to be the best chance we have. Sure it's dangerous, I know that; but so is staying here."

"I just think we're too young to die," she said.

"Who said anything about dying? This is going to work; you've just got to trust me."

I put my arms around her, and her head rested on my chest. And then, very softly, she began to cry. The stress of being in the underworld was pretty much the last straw. We never planned to visit ancient Greece, we hadn't asked for one hectic adventure after another, and we certainly didn't expect to risk our lives getting back to the land of the living. But here we were, stressed out and anxious; and finally it was too much. Lisa was totally defeated and ready to call it quits.

"If we ever get out of here," I said, "we'll become recluses. We'll sit on the front porch in our rocking chairs, recall our strange adventures in the ancient world, and we'll have a good laugh."

The crying stopped, and finally, she smiled.

When Persephone returned she described her plan to hijack Hades' chariot. "It's risky," she said, "but entirely feasible." The plan's success depended largely on the same knockout potion she prepared for Hades. Only this time she would enlist the aid of Kallista. The beautiful slave would dress provocatively, approach the horse guards, and offer them a drink with the promise of sexual pleasures to follow. However, before they could unhitch their loincloths, they would be snoring contentedly in the arms of Morpheus.

"Brilliant!" I said. "I can't imagine any red-blooded horseman resisting Kallista."

Our escape was scheduled for the following evening, and we were awake with apprehension much of that night. The following day flew by, and finally it was time to put the plan into action. Persephone had produced a pitcher filled with the powerful drug and a second pitcher, in the event of another accident. Kallista appeared looking absolutely ravishing. Her tunic was cut low to reveal as much cleavage as possible, and it was thigh length, which enhanced her long and curvaceous legs. Her dark hair was loose and fell gently over her shoulders. She was the absolute personification of sexual pleasure, and if our plan failed, it would certainly not be her fault.

We followed her to the stables and hid behind stacks of hay while she approached the horse guards. "I have brought some refreshment," she said. "And if you have the time, perhaps I can entertain you with some dancing and whatever other sensual activities might please you. I bring you a gift from my mistress, Queen Persephone."

The eyes of the four horse guards widened, and their chins nearly hit the ground. Who could blame them; Kallista was an astonishing sight. She virtually oozed sexuality.

"Many thanks to your mistress," said one of the guards. "You are a welcome sight."

The rest of the plan proceeded as successfully as one could only imagine. The horse guards eagerly ogled Kallista, while they drank the powerful potion, and in about three minutes they were out cold. Only one guard put a hand on her shoulder, and another reached for her waist, but that happened only moments before both collapsed to the ground.

"Okay," said Persephone, "let's go!"

We raced to the chariot, jumped aboard, and bolted out of the stable.

"Which way?" I shouted.

"Turn left here and follow the river," said Persephone. "And don't spare the horses," which I always thought was an expression from an old western movie. The four steeds galloped like the wind, and I began to feel like Ben Hur racing for my life. And then we heard the hounds.

"What's that?" I asked.

"Hades must have found us out. Faster!" she said. "Now quickly, turn right."

We raced at full speed for about twenty minutes before my arms began to ache. Lisa was right; I knew nothing about driving a chariot, and it was beginning to show. I could barely hang on.

"Are we near the opening?" I asked. Please let her say yes, I prayed.

"One more turn to the left, and we're there."

Suddenly, I saw clouds. What a thrill! And then we were climbing skyward.

"I see the moon," shouted Lisa over the thunder of the galloping hooves. "Don't stop now!"

With a final burst of energy our four black steeds broke through the underbrush and we were instantly back on earth. The horses were in a lather, and so—pretty much—was I. It had been a dynamic race to freedom, and we were exhausted. But we were also overjoyed.

"Well done," said Persephone. "I'll take it from here."

Lisa and I hugged Persephone. "You have our everlasting gratitude," I said. "I hope there will not be trouble with your husband."

"Don't worry about Hades; I can handle him," she said with confidence.

Persephone turned the chariot around and walked the horses back to the earthen opening. "Good luck to you both," she said. And then she smiled, waved, and disappeared from view.

We were finally back among the living and able to exhale. What a wonderful feeling.

SIXTEEN

It was the most fragrant evening I could remember. Compared with the underworld, which was dank and stale, the clear air was redolent with hyacinth, myrtle, and laurel. As we walked slowly back to our inn, the relief I felt being on earth overwhelmed me. I was reminded of something Winston Churchill once said, *"Nothing in life is so exhilarating as to be shot at without result."* We, too, had just dodged a bullet; and having successfully returned from the land of the dead it felt immensely satisfying.

"I've had enough excitement for a lifetime," said Lisa, which genuinely reflected my own feeling. "From now on, let's avoid any more grand adventures."

"Just one more," I said. "The grand adventure of returning to our own century and catching a plane back home."

"Okay, I'm ready for that."

"Do you think our marriage is ready for that?"

"I'd like to believe it is," she answered. "We may never achieve perfect harmony, but every alternative seems so much worse."

"So, you think we're stuck with each other?"

"Yes—but in a good way."

As we continued walking Lisa put her arm in mine and suddenly said "I love you, George, I really do, and I want us to be married forever."

I was stunned to hear words I had yearned to hear for longer than I could remember. I wanted to believe it was true, but how could I trust her? I wondered if her declaration of love might simply be the relief we both felt returning to earth. At that moment I, too, loved the whole world and everyone in it, but would I feel that way tomorrow? I was confused, and I said so.

"How can we ignore the last couple of years? How do we forget the quarrels, the heartaches, the lack of affection? How do we put all that behind us?"

There was a long silence before she said, "I don't really know. But I do know this: despite those times when I blamed you for my unhappiness, despite those difficult moments when I called you terrible names and acted like I hated you; despite all that, down deep in my heart I never stopped loving you. I know I haven't treated you very well, and for that, I am truly sorry.

"But why now? What prompted the change of heart at this very moment?"

"Things have changed, and it all seems so different." She appeared wistful.

"Different? What changed? What's different?"

There was another long pause before she said, "I may be pregnant."

I was shocked. Did I hear right? I didn't know what to say. We stopped walking, I took her in my arms, and we held each other for a long time. "I love you, too, Lisa, and I know I always will." Then I thought about Socrates and his walnut diet, and I suddenly laughed like a lunatic. "That wise old bastard was right. All I needed was a handful of walnuts. Wait 'til he hears we're going to be parents! He'll absolutely wet his pants; excuse me, I mean his tunic." We stood there for the longest time. We laughed until the laughter turned to tears; and then, as we remained in each other's arms, we both cried out of sheer joy. I don't think we had ever been happier.

We arrived at the inn feeling like conquering heroes. Zoe hugged us and said, "We were worried about you. We wondered how long a couple of meetings with long-dead heroes could possibly last. But here you are, and I must say, you both look pleased."

"It turned out to be more complicated than we assumed," I said, "and our plans changed once Hades discovered we had invaded his realm."

"How did you escape?" asked Elissa, who had joined the conversation.

"Nothing to it," said Lisa. "We swiped Hades' horses and chariot, and George drove us to freedom like the bravest and boldest charioteer you ever saw. He was an absolute hero!"

"That's mostly true," I said, "but we couldn't have done it without Persephone's help."

"The important thing," said Zoe, "is that you're here and you're safe." She was right; we were safe for now, but in ancient Greece how long would *that* last?

It had taken me a long time to realize this, but the history of the world, both ancient and modern, was the story of people not getting along. It was hardly a revolutionary thought, but it occurred to me years ago when I discovered that at any given moment there were dozens of major wars being waged simultaneously throughout the world. If you were to throw in quarrels, squabbles, and disagreements, like those between Lisa and me, I figured that ninety-eight percent of the world's population was currently angry with, or hostile towards, somebody—if not actually wishing them dead. The other two percent were in a state of transcendental meditation, or quite possibly unconscious.

So it was not surprising to learn that the Peloponnesian War had been in full swing for several years before we landed in ancient Greece.

I knew little about this historic war, other than the combatants were Athens and Sparta, the two most powerful Greek states. Both were closely allied against the Persian Empire during earlier attempted invasions. As allies, Athens took a leadership role as the major Greek naval power. Sparta, which had the foremost land-based military force, watched the growth of Athens' power with suspicion and concern. After defeating the Persians the two powers lost trust in one another, and that ultimately led to war.

We were completely unaware that a war was being waged, since fighting largely consisted of far-off naval battles and skirmishes outside the city walls. Within the city of Athens it was pretty much business as usual. One morning, however, Zoe mentioned that figs were in short supply because Spartan forces had destroyed much of the productive land around the city. Oddly, were it not for the fig shortage we might never have learned of the war.

Aphrodite also brought up the subject when she visited us later that day. "I know you're eager to return home," she said, "but getting you there has been complicated by the fighting between Athens and Sparta. The road on which you entered the city is often occupied by Spartan forces, and returning that way has become dangerous."

"So what are we to do?" I asked.

"I don't know," she answered. "We'll have to think about that."

I also thought about the problem and after several minutes said, "Recalling our arrival suggests to me a solution for our departure. After leaving the Athens Airport and driving for about twenty minutes, there was a point at which we suddenly stopped. A few moments later we met Doros, who brought us here in his donkey cart. Where our car stopped and Doros appeared is the exact place where modern Greece suddenly became ancient Greece. It seems to me we should head for that spot. So my question is this: where is it, and how do we get there?"

"There are several ways to reach that place," said Aphrodite, "but there is a risk of encountering Spartan forces regardless of which path one takes."

"But you're a powerful Greek goddess. Doesn't your sphere of influence include Sparta as well as Athens? What are you afraid of?"

"I'm afraid of what might happen to you. You are coming from Athens, and you will be considered the enemy. I can assure you, Spartan enemies are not treated well."

"After everything you went through to get us here, are you now going to let a few Spartans prevent us from returning home? I say pick the best path and let's find that spot. Otherwise, we could be stuck in ancient Greece forever, and that is totally unacceptable."

"Why the sudden impatience, George?"

"There is nothing further for us to do here, and Lisa needs the care of a modern doctor."

"Is she ill?"

"Only if you consider pregnancy an illness."

"Congratulations to you both!" she cried. "This is wonderful news! I will consider the situation and recommend a plan of action tomorrow. In the meantime, try to relax."

And that is what we did. We had Thea and Polona bathe us and wash away the last vestiges of the underworld aroma. Then we had a massage, an enjoyable meal, and by then we were ready for a peaceful afternoon nap. We slept right through the evening, and didn't stir until the sun began to rise the following morning.

Aphrodite appeared a bit later looking more beautiful than ever. I had almost forgotten how stunning she was. After our endless adventures I began to think of her impersonally as our wise guide and advisor. But here she was—a rare and genuine beauty. She was wearing a short toga, which revealed much of her flawless figure, and her long hair had been gathered into an attractive knot on top of her head.

"You are as delightful a sight as the sun rising over the hills," I said.

"Why, thank you, George That's very poetic. But what brought on that lovely compliment? Have you fallen in love with me?"

"Of course. Isn't every man in love with you? You are the very essence of sexuality and desire, and your beauty is legendary. By this time you must know you are irresistible."

"Yet, you resist me."

"Only because I constantly fight the impulse. However, I have discovered, through your efforts, a more powerful and enduring love—that for my wife. I will never forget what you did for us, and there will always be a place in my heart for you. In that sense, I will love you forever."

"I'm touched by your words, George."

We stood there silently for a long while, and then Aphrodite said, "I have an idea how you might return to the proper time and place of your previous life."

"Well, let's hear it," I said.

"We must convince the Spartans you are foreigners, not Athenians and not enemies. In that way we may avoid the danger. I suggest you put on those odd costumes you were wearing when you arrived. No one would suspect you were anything other than alien visitors with a bizarre sense of fashion. Spartans could not possibly assume you were a threat to them—unless, of course, your appearance frightened them."

"Frightened them?" I said. "How could a sport coat or pantsuit frighten them?"

"Perhaps not by your standards, but by our standards your apparel is quite bizarre."

"Well, we have to ditch the tunics in any event or they'll never let us on the plane. Togas and sandals in the twenty-first century are strictly for frat parties on Halloween."

"One more thing, George, your Athenian accent is so perfect you must try to change it so that no Spartan will doubt you are a foreigner. Can you do that?"

"I don't know; since I thought we were speaking English, what can I do?"

"Do you know any other language?"

"Just a few words in several languages, but not enough to really communicate."

"How about this?" suggested Lisa. "We can affect a backwoods accent, you know, like we're from Tennessee or Arkansas."

"I'm not familiar with that," said Aphrodite. "How does it sound?"

"It ain't rally anotha langwich, but dag nabbit, it's shore nearbout enuff to plumb fool anyone who ain't ever heard it. Ahm just sayin'."

Aphrodite smiled and said, "I'm not sure I understood you, but it sounded considerably less Greek, which should help identify you as a foreigner. I'm sure it will work."

"Right now," she said, "you might want to prepare for your departure and visit those to whom you wish to say goodbye."

Lisa agreed we should visit Socrates, since he was primarily responsible for our sudden change of fortune. When he opened his front door he beamed with genuine delight.

"I thought I might never see you two again," he said.

"We wouldn't think of leaving Athens without saying goodbye," I said. "We have come not only to thank you for your efforts on our behalf, but to tell you that your suggestion about walnuts has—to put it poetically—borne fruit."

"Would you repeat that?" he asked. "My hearing is getting worse by the day." I repeated my message and emphasized the part about walnuts bearing fruit.

"So your incapacity has suddenly improved?" he asked.

"Sufficiently for us to celebrate the anticipated arrival of a new family member."

"Well, congratulations! It seems I was right; love has indeed found a way. How wonderful. And what of your proposal to name the child after me?"

"Absolutely," said Lisa. "Our baby's name shall begin with the letter S, in your honor."

Socrates seemed pleased, and I suddenly became sad when I realized this remarkable mortal had only a few more years to live. It was a story that was well documented, but one I could not reveal to a man I had come to admire and respect. In a short time he would be tried and condemned to die by drinking poison hemlock. The official reason Socrates fell from grace was that he corrupted the minds of Athenian youths, but disapproval of him actually began when the Delphic Oracle proclaimed that no Greek was wiser than he. This was a genuine paradox, since Socrates believed he possessed no wisdom whatsoever.

To refute the Oracle's pronouncement, Socrates questioned the renowned poets, statesmen, and artisans of Athens only to discover that—although they thought themselves wise—they were not. He finally understood the Oracle's decision. Realizing that he himself was not wise, he actually was the wisest, because he was the only one aware of his own ignorance. Thus, those he publicly questioned began to look foolish and immediately turned against him. That led to the accusations of wrongdoing, subsequent trial, and eventual death.

As Socrates faced death he was heard to say, *"The hour of departure has arrived, and we go our way; I to die, and you to live. Which is better? Only the gods know."*

As Lisa and I left him, his words to us were, "Enjoy yourselves—it is later than you think." I wanted to say, "The very same to you, old friend."

I was unable to speak on our walk home, but I did shed a tear for the dear man, the wisest philosopher and most compassionate person I ever met.

SEVENTEEN

It was Sir Francis Bacon, the sixteenth century philosopher, who first said *Knowledge is Power*. That thought came to mind when I considered how I outwitted Ares and Hermes. Though they both had superior strength and godlike powers, I had twenty-first century wisdom, while they were stuck in the fifth century BC. And trading an electric toothbrush for Elissa's freedom could never have happened without modern-day knowledge. It wasn't exactly rocket science, but I did have the advantage of twenty-five centuries of civilization. So it occurred to me that if we happened to bump into hostile Spartans, a little knowledge about them should be helpful.

Zoe mentioned that Elissa spent time in Sparta, because her slave master had business dealings there. So I began by asking her to describe her thoughts about the place.

"My entire experience of being a slave was dreadful," she began, "but the worst part was the few months I spent in Sparta. Their entire culture is based on the military, and all they seem to care about is fighting wars. They are obsessed with power, and there is little else that interests them. As a result, Spartans are superior soldiers—fearless, skilful, and fiercely loyal to the state. But they are not particularly interesting or cultured people."

"Are you saying they have no philosophy or poetry or art as one finds in Athens?"

"None that I ever saw," she replied. "Spartans believe in discipline and austerity, and held in highest esteem seems to be the ability to endure hardship."

"It sounds like a terrible place," I said.

"Terrible only if you believe in freedom. To live in Sparta is to be rigidly controlled from birth to death. To begin with, infants who are weak or puny are abandoned and left to die. That really happens; I have seen it. Boys who survive until the age of seven are taken from their families to live in military barracks where they are taught discipline, survival skills, and ways of enduring pain and discomfort. At the age of twenty they become soldiers and either go into battle or continue to live with those with whom they trained. One is committed to a military life until the age of sixty, or more probably, until he is wounded or killed in battle. One more thing, Sparta is the only Greek state without protective city walls. They say, 'Our men are our walls.'"

It was difficult to understand how the two most powerful Greek states could differ in such an essential way. Though a mere hundred and fifty miles separated them, their cultures were a million miles apart. I had no reason to doubt Elissa's facts, as she was sensitive and bright and her assessment was convincing. Learning that much about the Spartans should have eased my apprehension, but in fact, it made me more nervous than ever.

Aphrodite appeared late that morning with plans for our departure. "You shall leave this evening," she said, "and travel with darkness as your cover. Will you be ready?"

"We were ready days ago," said Lisa. "This evening is none too soon."

"Doros will be here after sunset, and you shall travel by donkey cart to the spot where you first met. From there you must walk a few meters to the modern road that originally brought you to ancient Greece. I hope you will not encounter any enemy soldiers, but if you do, you must declare that you were visiting friends in Athens and are now returning to your home. Do you understand? You must insist that you have no political interests in this war and that you are completely neutral."

"That happens to be true," I said. "I believe most wars are foolish, and this one seems particularly pointless."

"I shall not be with you," Aphrodite continued, "as I do not wish to hinder your chance of success."

""But wouldn't your being there be an advantage to us?" asked Lisa.

"Not necessarily. Spartan warriors are famous for their single-minded purpose and dedication to the military. Devotion to gods runs a distant second; it is not nearly as compelling a force as their commitment to military power. My presence would only be a distraction. On the other hand, with good fortune, you may avoid confrontation; so let us think positively."

We spent the afternoon preparing for our journey back to the twenty-first century. We bathed, ate our last meal, and rested on our leaf-filled mattress, an unconventional comfort I had grown to appreciate. Oddly, since sleeping on dried leaves I had awakened each morning without stiffness or the slightest ache. Lisa agreed that she had never slept as soundly as she had in our primitive Grecian bed. It was an idea we considered investigating once we returned home. God knows, the trees in our back yard dropped enough leaves each year to fill a dozen mattresses.

Finally, we put on the familiar clothes we wore when arriving in ancient Athens. After wearing nothing but loose tunics for such a long time, a shirt and pants felt strangely confining. And underwear felt so inhibiting I considered going rogue, until Lisa strongly suggested I reconsider. The most seriously uncomfortable part of returning to modern life was exchanging sandals for shoes. I could swear that my feet were at least two sizes larger than when we arrived in Greece.

As the sun began to set behind the surrounding hills we began our farewells. I held Zoe's hand and said, "We will never forget you and your kind hospitality. You have made us most welcome here, and we are grateful for all you have done."

We hugged and kissed goodbye as she responded, "I will miss you both. You have been wonderful guests, and you have made our life at the inn interesting and exciting. We will remember you fondly."

Elissa hugged me and again thanked me for obtaining her freedom. "You have given me life as though you were my real father," she said. "And I will never, ever forget your kindness." And then she began to cry.

"There is nothing to be sad about," I said. "No one has ever deserved freedom more than you. You are bright and charming, and you represent the dignity and independence of free people everywhere. I am sure your life will be a happy one from now on."

Polona and Thea, our two slaves, were also tearful when we said goodbye. "It will not be the same here without you," said Thea. You have brought us excitement and delight. I am only sorry we never had a chance to learn about that activity called roll-in-the-hay."

"I'm sure George is sorry as well," said Lisa, "but that might have created complications."

"Oh, I don't know," I said. "Maybe there's still time before we leave."

"Don't make waves, dear," she said smiling. "Let's stop while we're ahead."

Finally, we faced Aphrodite. "We did not ask to be in ancient Greece," I said. "And as you can imagine, it has been a seismic shock to our systems. I'm still not sure why we were selected for your experiment, but I'm awfully glad we were. It could not have worked out more happily. We will always be grateful to you for our new relationship, our family to be, and for our bright future. You have also provided the most extraordinary and unforgettable adventure one could imagine. Not least of all, knowing you has been the highlight of our visit. Most people doubt that mythological gods existed, but you have proved otherwise, and we have developed a genuine love and appreciation for you."

"Thank you for those kind words, George. Let me say that you two were selected because you are special people. You have earned a second chance at happiness because you represent the ideals of our classic culture. This was not a gift to you, it was an opportunity; and fortunately, you made the most of it. I am proud of you both, and I wish you great happiness in your future."

Then we hugged and kissed and said our final farewells. Lisa had tears in her eyes as she climbed into Doros's donkey cart, and I was unable to speak. We waved goodbye, and set off on what I hoped was our final adventure. As we headed south, Doros's faithful donkey trotted along with confidence, as if he had made this journey many times before. Doros, who had remained quiet while we said our goodbyes, now began to chat like we were old chums off on a camping trip.

"I hope you are comfortable," he began, "because we are traveling a roundabout route to our destination, and it will take some time."

"How much time?" asked Lisa.

"Perhaps two hours, maybe more. The donkey and I will do our best."

I wasn't too concerned about Doros; he seemed experienced and focused on his assignment. The donkey, however, had me worried. I knew absolutely nothing about donkeys, or most other four-legged creatures, for that matter, but I noticed that the donkey's gait was uneven. If I were to guess, I'd say he was favoring his left hind leg. I had no idea the age of the animal, but I sincerely hoped he was not literally on his last leg.

"Doros," I said, "your donkey seems to be limping. Is he all right?"

"I hope so," he answered. "Old Nestor is getting on in age, but he's never failed me so far." That was like saying you never had a flat tire just before getting your first flat tire.

"Nestor?" Lisa asked. "Where did that name come from?"

"He was named after the oldest and wisest warrior who fought during the Trojan War."

"Well let's hope he has one more battle left in him," she said.

We sat back and tried to relax on the uncomfortable wooden planks. We bumped along over the rocky terrain, with both donkey and cart appearing creakier than an old ship in a squall at sea. After a couple of hours I asked Doros if we were anywhere near our destination. It was such a dark, moonless night I wondered if he even knew where on earth we were.

"I think we're getting close," he said. "But I can't be absolutely sure." That was not very reassuring. For all I knew we could have been going in circles.

Suddenly, Nestor, the old warrior donkey, began to cough; a few snorts at first, then a series of honks and wheezes. It sounded like a car with engine trouble, and like a problematic car, Nestor suddenly stopped moving. Oh no, I thought, don't tell me we're never going to see home again because of an ailing donkey. After all we've been through this just didn't seem fair.

Doros climbed down from his perch to inspect his sick animal. By this time Nestor's tongue was sticking out, and there was a string of mucous running from his nose.

"This is not good," said Doros. "Nestor seems to have a breathing problem."

"If he doesn't get better soon," I said, "we're all going to have a breathing problem."

Ignoring my comment Doros took a pail of water from the cart and encouraged Nestor to drink. After the poor animal took a few laps the coughing stopped, but he seemed to have no further inclination to move. I have no idea what goes through a donkey's mind, but I imagined him saying, "Hold on there, boys, don't get your tunics in a twist. I'm doing my best and just need to catch my breath." But Nestor said no such thing; he just stood there, stoic and motionless. Just like us.

"What are we to do?" asked Lisa. "It's the middle of the night, we have no idea where we are, our transportation has broken down, and hostile Spartans could be anywhere. I don't want to be an alarmist, but I think we have a problem."

"Do not worry," said Doros, who seemed inexplicably cheerful. "I will get you to your destination, even if I must carry you there." Big talk, I thought, from our four-foot-tall Munchkin.

Lisa and I strolled over the rough terrain to get the kinks out of our legs, while Doros remained with his ailing donkey. He carried on a conversation with Nestor, the purpose of which was to convince the poor creature that he had an obligation to get well, and to do so soon— or else. However, if the dumb animal actually had respiratory problems as well as a bum leg, Doros was whispering into a gale-force wind.

After a half hour I suggested to Doros that perhaps, since we were so close to our destination, we could walk the rest of the way.

"Not a bad idea," he said. "But what shall I do about Nestor? He refuses to move."

"Nestor, Shmestor," I said, "your first obligation is getting us home. Your donkey will follow us or do whatever makes him happy. That cannot be our concern."

"But Nestor has been a faithful companion for nearly fifteen years. I cannot abandon him."

"Dammit, Doros, let's get our priorities straight. We have to get going right now!"

Just then we heard murmurs coming from a clump of trees to our right, "Shush!" I said; "someone else is here." And then without warning we heard the swish of a projectile. A spear landed within inches of where we stood, ricocheted off a rock, and grazed Nestor on his right rump. The poor beast let out a deafening roar as he bolted into the air. "Calm down," said Doros, but what living creature suddenly speared in the butt could possibly remain calm?

"Quickly!" said Doros, "get into the cart! Hurry, now!"

Lisa and I leaped into the cart, and Nestor took off like he was running toward the finish line of the Kentucky Derby. Four soldiers, whom we assumed were Spartans, were chasing us on foot. Even though they were remarkably fast, Nestor was moving like a guided missile, bum leg, respiratory problem, and all. I'm sure we were going at least thirty miles an hour, and within a few moments we had outdistanced the Spartans.

"That was a close call," said Lisa. "Much too close for comfort."

"Doros," I said, "we must get to our destination as quickly as possible, not only for our own safety, but poor Nestor is still losing blood."

"I think I see the spot directly ahead," he said. "There is the tree where we first met."

"Thank God!" said Lisa.

Doros guided the cart toward the tree and pulled the reins to stop Nestor. The suffering beast gave a final wheeze and sank to his knees. He truly looked done for. Doros jumped out of the cart, rushed to the donkey, and threw his arms around him. "Don't give up now," he pleaded. He offered Nestor some water, and the dazed beast weakly lapped it up. At that moment it was anyone's guess whether he would survive.

Just then a Spartan soldier in full battle regalia came out from behind the tree and said, "Stay right where you are." Then he asked, "Who are you people, and what are you doing here?"

Remembering the country accent I began, "Mah wife and me am vistors to yo cuntry," I said. "We just goin to ah home. And ah drivah be a slave from Athens. We is in a big hurry, so please stand asahd so that we can git on ah way."

"Not so fast, stranger; I need to know a bit more about you."

So there we were, a few meters distant from the twenty-first century; but crossing the finish line remained in doubt. I began to wonder if this odyssey would *ever* end.

EIGHTEEN

The soldier was large, muscular, and armed to the teeth, so to speak—a formidable sight if there ever was one. He wore a molded breastplate, which made him appear like a comic book superhero, a metal helmet with cheek plates, and shin armor that extended from below the knees to the ankles. He also sported a scarlet cape, which identified him as a Spartan. There was a large bronze shield in one hand, a spear in the other, and a short sword at his waist. I figured that with all that paraphernalia he probably weighed a few hundred pounds. He also gave the impression that he could single-handedly challenge the entire Athenian army and likely win.

Referring to the large shield, Elissa had mentioned that Spartan warriors were told, "Come home *with* this shield or *upon* it." In other words, if you can't return victorious, then come home dead. So this is what we faced—the pathetically defenseless architect and his pregnant wife versus a human battleship. David and Goliath came to mind, but there I was, without sling or stone.

The soldier asked why we were wandering around this uninhabited area. I explained that we were heading home, but our donkey became ill before we reached our destination. "Where is your destination?" he wanted to know. I couldn't very well say the Athens International Airport, as that wouldn't exist for another twenty-five hundred years. So I said, "The Yew'nited States."

"I've not heard of that place," he said.

"It's a fer piece from here, yonder 'cross a whole lotta oshun," I said.

"And what were you doing in Athens?" he asked.

"Visitin' frens."

"Are your Athenian friends involved in this war?"

"No siree, Bob. They's mostly artists an' philosopher-type people. They hate war sumpton awful. Why they'd rather do anathin' else than go kill folks."

"And you? Do you hate war, too?"

"Ah plumb *do* hate war more than anythin'. You bet ah do! Ah think war is just about the mos' dumb-ass way o' settlin' problems. Ah think yo oughta tawk out yo differnts and not rush inta anythin' that gonna hurt folks. I surely do." I could tell by the look on Lisa's face that I had gone a bit overboard. Her expression said, "Dummy, you're talking to a Spartan soldier whose very purpose in life is waging war. What are you trying to do, get us shot at sunrise?"

So I backtracked a bit. "Don' get me wrong, Mr. Spartan soldier man, ah reckon sumtimes one's gotta do what one's gotta do, an folks like yo gotta fight for what yo believe is raiht. Bah the way, yung man, has yew got a name?"

"My name is Damanos, which means one who kills." Somehow, that didn't surprise me. "There is more we wish to know," he said, "so you will remain here until my commander returns."

"An' when's that?"

"Soon I hope, but you will be comfortable until that time. We will provide a tent for you."

"A tent? Whaddyall mean? We caint stay all night; we gotta be gitten."

"You will be released when *we* decide you may leave. Meanwhile, I will not bind you as a prisoner of war; but I warn you not to attempt an escape. If you do, I can assure you I will take great pleasure in separating your head from your body. So make yourself comfortable; this may take a while." I wondered how *anyone* could make himself comfortable after hearing such a dire warning.

Lisa and I were led to a small tent that contained a thin mattress of dried leaves, two blankets, a pitcher of water, and a dish of cheese and figs. The tent had no headroom, so we had to crawl in on our hands and knees.

"Not exactly the Savoy," said Lisa, "but let's hope we won't be here long."

I noticed that there were no more than eight Spartan soldiers in the group, so I suggested we might wait until most of them were asleep and then sneak out and climb the small hill leading to the airport road.

"Are you crazy?" she asked. "We were just warned that an attempted escape is a one-way ticket to decapitation. If you don't mind, I prefer my head exactly where it is."

"We can always say we had insomnia and were just taking a stroll."

"A stroll? Are you kidding? How stupid would these guys have to be to buy that story? Right now I'm going to have a snack and then take a nap. I suggest you forget a stroll and do the same."

Damanos awakened us two hours later to report that the commander had returned. "He wishes to speak to the prisoners," he said. Prisoners? Did I miss something? When did we officially become prisoners?

Damanos led us to a large tent that served as a military headquarters. It contained an array of spears, swords, knives, arrows, helmets and other personal armored items. Sitting at an elevated desk at the center of the tent, like an emperor on his throne, was the commander of this small military force. He was a good-looking, middle-aged Spartan with a full beard that was beginning to go gray and thick eyebrows that enhanced his fierce appearance. The commander also had a prominent scar that ran from the edge of his left eye, across his cheek, and ended at his chin. The left eye drooped a bit, producing an asymmetry to his otherwise handsome features.

"Who are you?" he asked brusquely.

"Mah name is George, and mah wife here is called Lisa." He gave me a quizzical look.

"That's enough, young man; you can drop the phony accent. One of my men heard you speaking in your tent and we know you speak flawless Greek. Why are you trying to mislead us?"

Caught red-handed, I wondered how to squirm out of the corner into which I had just painted myself. I decided to tell the truth.

"We were told that our speech might suggest we are Athenians, and that could not be further from the truth. We are, in fact, visitors to your country who are speaking our native language. However, strange this explanation may sound, whatever we say comes out in perfect Greek, without the trace of an accent. It is a mystery we cannot begin to understand or explain."

"Are you trying to insult my intelligence?" asked the incredulous commander.

"You may believe it or not, as you will, but it is the honest truth. We are from another time and another place."

"What time? What place?"

"If I told you, I guarantee you would not believe me."

"Tell me, and *I* shall decide."

"We are from a place called the United States, and our civilization is presently twenty five hundred years later than yours. We enjoy a life you could not begin to understand, we have machines and devices you would find astonishing, and the unconventional manner of dress you see is our least significant difference."

"You're right, I do not believe you. Have you any proof of these outrageous claims?"

"I have several ways to prove what I just told you. For example, what time of day would you say it is right now?"

"You know it is impossible to determine that; the sun has not yet risen."

"Yet, I can look at this device on my wrist and tell you that it is precisely 3:35 in the morning. I do not need the sun to tell me that. This device, called a wristwatch, can tell me the precise time, day or night. It also tells me the day of the month. Furthermore, I can read the time without light, as the numbers glow in the dark."

The commander came closer to inspect my Swiss Army watch. He looked at me with a puzzled look, but remained silent. I then reached into the pocket of my jacket where I had a small box of matches that I picked up at the Savoy Hotel in London. "How do you make fire?" I asked.

"What do you mean?"

"I mean, if you wanted to start a fire to warm yourself or cook food, how do you do it?"

"Every Spartan soldier carries flint and iron. You simply strike one against the other until they create a spark, and then you use that spark to ignite some tinder."

"And how long would you say that process takes?"

"An experienced soldier like myself can produce fire in fewer than three minutes."

"Well, get a load of this, Buster." I took out a single wooden match, struck it against the side of the box, and the match burst into flame. The entire action took only three *seconds*. The commander was literally speechless. He remained standing, wide-eyed, and with his mouth partially open. And there I stood feeling like Merlin, Houdini, and the Wizard of Oz rolled into one.

"Care to see any further proof?" I asked.

"What do you have in mind?"

"Please extinguish the oil lamps; I need total darkness."

"I warn you not to attempt an escape," said the commander.

"I assure you I will not," I replied. The lamps were snuffed out and I waited a moment for our eyes to dilate. Then I took from my pocket my light emitting diode flashlight. I switched it on and pointed its powerful beam at the commander's face.

"Begone, evil spirit!" he cried. "You have blinded me!" And then he began to babble as though the light had burned a hole in his brain. I turned off the light and the lamps were relit.

"Do you need any further proof of what I have told you?" I asked.

"No," he replied, "that won't be necessary. I have enough evidence to confirm that you are a genuine sorcerer. What I do not know, however, is against which side in this conflict you intend to work your evil magic."

"We take no side in your foolish war. We are neutral, peace loving, and oppose all armed conflict. Furthermore, what you have observed is neither magic nor evil. It is simply evidence of life in the twenty-first century."

"Nevertheless," said the commander, "you shall remain prisoners until we learn more about your activities."

I was beyond frustrated; the commander was convinced we were foreign sorcerers sent to cause trouble for the Spartans. On the other hand, since we were not accused of any specific crime, I thought I might appeal to his Hellenic sense of fair play. But apparently that would not happen today. He dismissed us by saying there were more pressing matters to attend to, and we were left to wait until the pressing matters were resolved.

"What can we do?" asked a disgruntled Lisa. "We can't very well spend the rest of the Peloponnesian War in a pup tent."

"That's true, but we don't have many options. I think they would love to see us attempt an escape just so they could hack us to pieces. Bloodthirsty bastards!"

A bit later in the morning we asked if we could visit Doros and his donkey. Both were resting in a shelter close to our tent. Nestor was covered by a blanket and looked weak, but content. Doros leaped up when we appeared and greeted us warmly. "How wonderful to see you again," he said. "I feel enormous guilt for having failed in my mission to deliver you safely to your destination. For that I am truly sorry."

"Do not blame yourself, Doros. You did your best, and although things didn't work out as planned we are well and will find another way to solve our problem. But tell us, how is Nestor?"

"He is recovering but is in no hurry to get back on the trail. The soldiers are treating him well; they give him water and allow him to roam for food. He is happy, I think."

"And you?"

"I am a slave with no great expectations. But I trust everything will work out."

Lisa and I strolled back towards our tent. The day was beautiful, the weather perfect, and the landscape appeared austere but peaceful. One would never guess there was a war going on, nor could we believe we were prisoners in a conflict about which we knew little and cared even less.

"I have an idea," I said. "Perhaps there is a way to escape this place. We only have to reach that hill over there; it's not more than a quarter of a mile away. I'll bet we could run that distance in a couple of minutes."

"Yes, but it would take half that time for a Spartan spear to stop us. How do you propose we reach that hill without attracting attention?"

"We wait until dark," I said, "when most of the Spartans are asleep. Then we get Nestor, who apparently has complete freedom to roam for food. We have him stroll towards the hill, while the two of us hide beneath the blanket that covers him."

"Don't you think it might look odd seeing a donkey with a large humped back?"

"I admit it's risky, but I think it's worth trying. If we're discovered we'd be no worse off than we are now. After all, we've committed no crime and we've not been accused of anything."

"How about attempted escape? Then comes decapitation. End of story!"

"I think you're being overly pessimistic."

"Another thing," said Lisa. "I assume we leave the luggage behind; that's no big deal. But how can we be sure what's on the other side of the hill?"

"All we know—or at least hope—is that beyond the hill is the twenty-first century. It certainly was when we arrived. If that's the case, we can hitchhike, walk, or even crawl to the airport. At that point I don't really care. About the luggage, we'll buy a new wardrobe the first chance we get. That's a promise."

Before we reached our tent the Spartan, Damanos, stopped us to say the commander wished to see us right away. It felt as though we were being called to the principal's office again.

"Before you say anything," I began, "we wish to know if we are being accused of a crime and what particular crime that might be?"

"I am in charge here," bellowed the commander, "and I will ask the questions. How dare you presume to control this conversation?" His facial scar turned scarlet and appeared to throb to the rhythm of his elevated blood pressure.

"I meant no disrespect, sir, but I know something of your culture and how it values the laws that guide your citizens. I know that Greeks believe in liberty and respect for the individual. We are not citizens of your country, but we share your love of freedom and democracy. It seems reasonable to ask, therefore, why we are being held here against our will."

"Fair enough," said the commander. "I will answer that question. You are being held because we suspect you are aiding the Athenians. We are currently at war with Athens, and we cannot permit foreigners to support them in this fight against us. It is true we have not charged you with a specific crime; but before we release you we must be certain you pose no danger to Spartan forces."

"I have tried to assure you we have no interest in war, yours or anyone else's. We believe wars are generally stupid and unnecessary, and frankly, we do not care who wins or loses. In my opinion both Athens and Sparta have already lost. Just look at the number of deaths and the amount of destruction. Do you really believe that what you are doing is worth the incredible waste of life and fortune?"

"I believe it is."

"Of course; you would. Your life is dedicated to warfare. But do you think your mothers, wives, and daughters would agree?"

"I have no time to debate this issue," said the commander. "I only wish to know why you are here and what sorcery you have planned. And you will remain here until I can determine the answers to those questions."

"As we say in my country, commander, you are on the wrong track and definitely barking up the wrong tree. We are here because our donkey could go no further, I am not capable of sorcery, and we have absolutely no interest in your silly war. Every word I have spoken is to you is true, and that is all I can say."

I was now certain that the commander would keep us around until he was convinced we posed a threat, and then things would become worse. We could no longer ignore the mortal danger we faced by remaining here. We had to escape; we definitely had to make a run for it.

NINETEEN

Our plan to escape was now of paramount importance. I was convinced that the longer we remained Spartan prisoners the less likely we would ever see our home again. More importantly, Lisa would be deprived the medical care she would soon require.

Damanos appeared the following morning and said, "I hear you are a sorcerer. Is that true?"

"I've been called worse."

"Yes, but is it true?"

"It all depends; do you really want to know, or are you here simply to annoy me?"

"I just wondered how someone who is supposed to have amazing magical powers could allow himself to be captured."

"Are you doubting my amazing magical powers?"

"Well, here you are, a Spartan prisoner. That tells me—at the very least—you must be a fairly incompetent sorcerer."

"Be careful, Damanos; it might be a mistake to question my powers. If I wanted to make you disappear, believe me, you'd be gone by now. You are treading on eggshells, my friend." He began to look worried, but the taunting continued.

"Well, if you are so powerful why do you remain here?"

"An ordinary Spartan soldier, like you, cannot possibly understand me or the world I come from. But I assure you, I will soon be gone—without a trace—and you will forever wonder how that happened. In the meantime you would be wise to look over your shoulder every so often; you may be in greater danger than you think." The pompous Spartan walked away without another word, but I now knew that he feared me nearly as much as I feared him.

Our escape plan remained uppermost in my mind, but the longer I considered the risks the more I thought about the potential dangers. I wondered, for example, if we would be able to guide Nestor toward the hill as we lay on the donkey's back. How would the dumb animal even know where we wanted to go? At that point, it seemed prudent to discuss our escape plan with Doros.

"There are at least two good ways to guide Nestor toward the hill," he said. "The best way would be for me to lead him. I could walk along his side, as I often do, and gently nudge him in the proper direction. It would not attract much attention, because we are often seen walking together. The other way, which is somewhat riskier, would be to set down a path of Nestor's favorite shrub. There is one particular shrub he absolutely loves. If I were to lay down some branches of that shrub between here and the hill, he would follow the path without fail. However, your escape might take quite a long time, as he eats at his own pace. And there is always the chance he would become satisfied and stop eating before reaching the hill."

I discussed Doros's suggestions with Lisa later that day.

"Basing our escape on Nestor's digestive system," she said, "seems precarious, to say the least. The only idea that makes sense is to have him guide the donkey, but that would put him in great danger. I hate to involve him in all this, because if we fail it will be the end of us all."

"Yes, but if we attempt to escape without his help there's a good chance Nestor will simply ignore us, wander in whatever direction he pleases, and it will still be the end of us."

I wasn't sure what to do, but I knew our days were numbered and we had to escape soon. I became further convinced we had to act quickly when the commander informed me we were moving.

"Our work here is done," he said. "We have surveyed the area and found it free from enemy forces, except of course, for you. So we will be moving to another location tomorrow morning. You will be taken with us, since you are prisoners of war."

"I am sorry to disappoint you, commander, but we cannot go with you," I said. "First of all, we are not prisoners of war, as you claim, since we are not at war with you. Secondly, we must return to our home, which was our original destination."

"Please understand this," said the commander in his most solemn tone. "You will go with us, or you will end up in the realm of Hades. Those are your choices!"

"Are you saying you would rather kill us than allow us to go home? Are you serious? You would actually murder us, even without evidence that we are a danger to you?"

"Yes, that is exactly what I am saying. Do not doubt for a moment that is what will happen."

So there we were, some four hundred yards—once around the track—from the twenty-first century. But we were about to be moved in the opposite direction from the finish line. Our choice was clear; we must act immediately.

"Tonight's the night," I said to Lisa. "The Spartans are moving tomorrow morning, and they intend to take us with them. So tonight we head for the hill and freedom. I will inform Doros."

I said to the slave, "We are leaving tonight and we thank you for all you have done and are about to do for us."

"I only wish it could be more," he replied. "What time do we leave?"

"We will wait until all but the nighttime guards are asleep. That should be well after midnight. Prepare Nestor and don't forget the blankets. I intend to set our tent on fire in order to distract the guards. That will be your signal. As the Spartans rush to the fire you and the donkey will proceed to the tree where we first met. Lisa and I will be waiting there, ready to hop aboard and trot away. With fire as our diversion, we hope to minimize the risk."

"You can count on me," our miniature collaborator replied.

It sounded so logical, so easy; yet I knew there was much that could go wrong. The most difficult part of the plan was waiting for the day to end. Somehow the afternoon seemed endless; I thought the sun would never set. But finally it did, leaving a spectacular red sky that gradually turned to black. Lisa and I chose the clothes we would wear, as we regretted leaving the rest of our things. I took only the essentials: passports, wallet, flashlight, and a small knife I picked up in Athens. If anyone got dangerously close I was prepared to give him a few perforations to remember us by.

I wanted to nap but feared we might oversleep, so we remained awake and alert. At about three o'clock in the morning I decided to act. The camp was so still I could hear soldiers snoring.

"Time to go," I said. Lisa crawled out of our tent and slowly walked toward the tree. I slit open our mattress and spread out the dried leaves. This ought to go up like fireworks on the Fourth of July, I thought. What an appropriate celebration of freedom this will be! I struck a match threw it onto the dry leaves, and dashed toward the tree. Smoke was rising from the tent as I raced away, and two minutes later, as I reached the tree, flames began to leap skyward. Doros and Nestor appeared moments later.

We hopped aboard the donkey and lay face down, while Doros covered us with a large blanket. At that same moment we heard a guard yell, "Fire!" By that time the tent was fully engulfed in flames, and we were trotting towards the hill. Doros poked Nestor, who began to pick up speed as a result of the prodding. Soon Doros was running to keep up with the donkey.

One of the soldiers said, "Be quiet; I think I hear a horse galloping."

"There are no horses here," said the commander. "But there is a donkey! Quick, look in the shelter to see if the slave and his donkey are still there."

Two soldiers with torches ran to the shelter.

"They are gone!" one cried. "Neither the slave nor the donkey is here!"

Damanos said, "He definitely is a sorcerer! He promised he would vanish without a trace, and he has taken the slave and the animal with him. They have all gone up in flames!"

"I don't believe that," said the commander. "Let us search the area."

By this time we had reached the foot of the hill. Lisa and I slid off Nestor's back and I said to Doros, "This is where we leave you, my friend. We will run up the hill alone. Many thanks for your help, and may all your gods bless you."

"Doros had tears in his eyes as he said, "Godspeed to you!"

We raced up the short hill and waved goodbye. At that moment two Spartan soldiers appeared and grabbed Doros. "What do you want?" he asked.

"What are you doing out here?"

"Nestor wanted to stroll and nibble some grass, so I took him for a walk."

"Where are your Athenian friends?"

"How am I to know such a thing? They are probably sleeping."

"Not likely; their tent just burned to the ground."

"Oh, what a tragedy," said Doros. "Were they hurt?"

"No, you fool; they have vanished."

"Well, what do you expect me to do about that? I know nothing of magic."

"Tell us where they are or I'll slay you this instant," said one soldier.

"I swear I know nothing," cried Doros. "You must believe me!"

I had heard enough. I knew the Spartans were vicious and ruthless. There was no doubt in my mind they would get the truth out of Doros or kill him in the process. I had to do something. Lisa grabbed my arm. "Be careful," she said.

I moved slowly down the hill toward the group with my flashlight in a pocket and the small knife in my right hand. Then I noticed a dead branch on the ground; it was about the size of a Louisville Slugger. This is better than a knife, I thought. I picked up the thick branch, put the knife in my belt, and continued down the hill.

As I came within a branch length of the soldier holding Doros I cried, "Let go of him, you miserable bully!" Simultaneously, I pulled out the flashlight and pointed it at the soldier's face, which had just turned in my direction. He dropped Doros and raised his shield to ward off the blinding light. Then I gripped the branch and swung it like a major leaguer aiming at a low ball below the knees. I caught him squarely in the shins, and he howled in pain. His shin guards flew in the air and he dropped his shield. This gave me the chance to pull out my knife and plunge it into his side. He fell to the ground writhing like a wounded animal.

Meanwhile, Doros was whacking the other soldier with his short whip, which appeared no more effective than a fly swatter. The soldier turned and threw his spear in my direction. I ducked, but the spear grazed the upper part of my left arm. Without another thought I swung the dead branch at his head. My efforts produced nothing more than a sizable dent in his helmet. However, the force of the blow propelled him into Nestor, who until that moment was standing quietly minding his own business. The enraged donkey turned, bucked, and threw back his hind legs in a kick that sent the Spartan several feet into the air. No other creature in the animal kingdom could have landed a more forceful blow. The stunned soldier landed like a meteor that had just fallen to earth.

As he lay there unconscious I said to Doros, "Now's your chance. Take Nestor and go before the others get here." He gave me a hug, jumped upon Nestor's back, and the two galloped off in the opposite direction.

Meanwhile my wounded left arm was dripping blood from the spear wound. I approached the unconscious Spartan, tore off a long strip of his scarlet cape, and bound my wound. The arm continued to throb, but I staunched the bleeding. I raced back up the hill and in a few moments was wrapped up in Lisa's arms.

"What happened down there?" she asked. "All I heard were sounds of a struggle. Are you okay? And what happened to Doros?"

"I'll tell you everything, but be quiet now; I hear soldiers coming."

We stood in the dark at the top of the hill and heard every word of the conversation below.

"Here they are, commander. Ariston is unconscious, and Podargos is bleeding, but he is still alive. It looks like there was a fight, but I see no evidence of the enemy. Who on earth could have done this?"

"I would guess it was the Athenian captives," said the commander.

"But didn't they die when their tent caught fire?"

"I doubt it. I suspect they started the fire to divert us, and then they escaped."

"Shall we search the area?"

"Not much point," said the commander. "They've had too much time to get away. I don't believe we would find them."

The other soldiers placed the two wounded warriors on their shields and carried them back towards their camp. By now the distant tent fire had become an ember glowing in the dark. The commander's last words were spoken with considerable bitterness. "Perhaps he was telling the truth after all; there was something foreign about that odd couple. We will never know whether or not he was a genuine sorcerer, but in any case, I say good riddance."

Lisa and I did not dare move before the military party was some distance away. For the first time in a long time we breathed easier and felt a small degree of safety.

"What happened to your arm?" she asked worriedly. "That bandage is dripping blood."

"I ran into a Spartan spear," I said. "It's only a flesh wound—really nothing."

Nevertheless, she took off her scarf and wrapped it tightly over the piece of scarlet cape. Then she said, "Where to now, my Peloponnesian hero?"

"Well," I replied, "if we walk down this hill, according to my theory, we ought to find some evidence of the twenty-first century. And if my calculations are correct, the Athens International Airport ought to be straight ahead. But if I'm wrong . . ."

"Don't even think about that," she said. "C'mon, time to go home."

TWENTY

As we began to walk down the hill I was struck by the beauty of the night. There were a million stars overhead, and the air was moist and warm. There was a feeling of serenity I had not felt for longer than I could remember. But what was it that just happened? The recent memory of my battle with Spartan soldiers was like a bad dream from which I just awoke. Did it actually happen? Was it real? I was a peace-loving guy; I knew nothing about combat or war and—least of all—could I ever imagine plunging a knife into the flesh of another human being. That was totally inconceivable. So how could I begin to understand the extraordinary event that just took place? I suppose it was no more bizarre than meeting a mythological god, speaking to an ancient philosopher, or our implausible visit to the underworld. None of that made any sense either. No sense at all. None of it!

As I tried putting those memories into context I noticed a dramatic change in the surface on which we were walking. I could swear it looked like a paved road. I switched on my flashlight and could not believe what I saw. The surface had a faded white line down the center. Then it hit me. This couldn't possibly be an ancient Greek roadway; this had to be something out of the twenty-first century. I suddenly heard the remote hum of an engine. I looked up and saw in the distance the flashing lights of a plane. It was half a mile above us, but it was definitely an airplane.

"Hallelujah!" I cried.

"We did it!" exclaimed Lisa. "Thank God, we made it back!"

We stopped walking, hugged one another, and shed tears of relief. "I knew we'd eventually return to the proper century," I said, "but there was always a speck of doubt that kept me up nights."

"And I always believed you *would* get us back," said Lisa. "Really, George, you're an honest-to-god superhero. By comparison, those mythological heroes look pretty pathetic."

We continued walking arm in arm on the pavement that, strangely, was completely devoid of traffic. We walked for another twenty minutes before I suddenly remembered my cell phone. During our stay in ancient Greece that miraculous device was about as useful as a microwave oven. I recalled the total absence of phone service when we first arrived, but since we were now somewhat closer to the airport, could there possibly be service here?

I turned on the phone and after several seconds I heard a beep.

"It works," I cried. "Who should I call?"

"How about getting us a taxi?" suggested Lisa. I dialed the help line, a number I had programmed into my phone on our arrival in Greece, and I asked to be connected to a taxi service. A man answered the call speaking Greek. It was a language I had not heard since arriving at the Athens International Airport.

"Do you speak English?" I asked.

"A little," he answered with a strong accent.

"We need a taxi," I said.

"This is a limousine service."

"Okay, that's even better. Can you send a limousine?"

"Where are you?"

"I'm not sure, but it's somewhere on the road between the Airport and the city."

"Stay where you are and I shall attempt to track your location."

I held on for several minutes before the dispatcher returned. During that time I noticed that, after a long period of neglect, my phone battery was about to expire.

"I have sent someone to pick you up," he said. "You are about thirty kilometers from the airport. A driver should be there within a half hour."

I shut off the phone and breathed a hopeful sigh of relief. Thirty minutes later I saw headlights approaching. We stood at the side of the road and I began to wave my powerful flashlight. The vehicle slowed and finally stopped. Out jumped the driver who said, "Good God! I'm in shock! I had no idea we would ever meet again. But here you are, just as I left you."

"*You're* shocked? How do you think *we* feel seeing the very person who abandoned us without explanation or even a proper goodbye?"

It was, of course, Alexandros, our limousine driver from what seemed months ago.

"This is positively eerie," I said. "You were the last person we saw on our way to the city and now the first person we see as we return. Why have you returned to the scene of the crime?"

"Crime? What crime?" he asked. "I work for a transportation company and go where they tell me to go. I transport passengers from here to there and mind my own business. What is the crime in that?"

"Well, in case you forgot, let me remind you what happened. When we were last together you stopped the car, removed the key, and walked away. You abandoned us. You insisted you could not take us to our hotel in Athens. So you left us to our own devices. I'd like to know why. How could you do such a thing?"

"I was only following orders and I did as I was told."

"Told by whom?"

"I receive text messages from our office. There is no name attached to these messages. I simply assume they come from my superiors."

"And so someone told you to dump two American tourists in the middle of nowhere? Is that what you're saying? Sorry, pal, I don't buy that. But even if it were true, didn't you care what happened to us? Didn't you feel any personal responsibility?"

"I was assured you would be all right. I did care what happened to you, and I asked the same question you are asking now. I was told you would be cared for. Didn't that happen? Didn't someone meet you just a few meters from where I left you?"

"That's not the point. You deserted us and acted irresponsibly."

There was a long silence before Alexandros said, "I am truly sorry for causing you concern. I never meant to make you feel uneasy, but now I can understand how you must have suffered. I hope you will forgive me and allow me to take you to your next destination."

"How do I know we can trust you?"

"You absolutely can. I am at your service and will take you wherever you wish to go."

"Well," said my practical wife, "I'd like to visit the nearest ladies room. You have no idea how long I've waited for this."

Lisa's urgent request ended the discussion. We drove off and within a few minutes arrived at a small highway rest stop that featured gas pumps, rest rooms, a snack bar, and other amenities. Compared to ancient Greece, it looked like an elegant five-star resort. As Lisa rushed to the first flush toilet she had seen in weeks, I ordered a chilled glass of ouzo at the snack bar. When Lisa returned she ordered an espresso. So there we sat, happily chatting and enjoying, like never before, benefits of the twenty-first century that were formerly taken for granted.

"I cannot tell you how much I've missed a good cup of coffee," she said, "not to mention a toilet that flushes and enough toilet paper to gift wrap an elephant."

After another half hour we decided to continue our journey to the Airport. We looked for Alexandros, but he was nowhere to be found. I checked the men's room and finally walked out to the parking lot. The limousine was gone. I went back inside and asked the attendant if he knew what happened to our driver.

"He drove away with two men a short while ago," he answered.

"Two men? Who were they?"

"I have no idea. He told me to let you know he was leaving, and that you should not worry. He was taking care of business, and what he was doing would be best for you. Incidentally, the two men were large and looked like bodyguards. They claimed that Hades had sent them here. I guess that was supposed to be a joke. They looked for you, but unfortunately, they failed to check the snack bar. The driver said something to them, and they all hurried away."

I was thoroughly confused. I truly believed we were finished with ancient Greek intrigue. I innocently thought that returning to the twenty-first century would end our classic adventures and bring us some peace of mind. But apparently I was wrong. It seems that Hades was still upset by our clandestine visit to the underworld and still hungered for revenge. He must now realize we used his palace to hide out, right under his nose, actually. And then there was the matter of borrowing his chariot and horses to escape. That only added insult to injury. Of course, he might have taken out some frustration on his wife, Persephone, who helped us every step of the way. But he probably figured a couple of mortals were easier targets. So apparently he sent a couple of henchmen to rough us up, or possibly he had something more deadly in mind.

On the other hand what could they do to us? We were now back in the twenty-first century, not the perilous days of the fifth century B.C. There were laws here to protect people and police to enforce the laws. I didn't know what danger we might be in, but I didn't want to wait to find out. For all I knew, Hades and his chariot—or even Spartan soldiers—could be waiting around the next curve in the road.

"Can you call a taxi for us?" I asked the attendant.

"Of course," he answered, "but first, you might want to change that bandage on your arm; it is dripping blood. Are you badly hurt?"

"Just a flesh wound," I answered. "Have you a first aid kit?"

The attendant produced a kit and proceeded to unwrap my bandage. "First we'll put on an antiseptic," he said. "By the way, how did you get hurt?"

"If I told you I'm sure you wouldn't believe my story."

"Tell me anyway."

"My wound came from an ancient Spartan spear. And the bandage you just removed was a piece of fabric torn from a Spartan soldier's cape."

"Okay," he said, "I get it. It's none of my business." By the time my arm was re-bandaged the taxi arrived and we were back on the road to the Airport.

"What will we do?" asked Lisa. "Apparently, Hades isn't going to give up."

"I'm not sure," I answered. "I don't know how much power he actually has here, but I think we should get on a plane and leave Greece as quickly as we can."

"Could he possibly follow us to California?"

"Who knows? I never heard of such a thing, but then again, I never believed it was possible to visit ancient Greece."

We sat quietly, lost in our anxieties, as our taxi sped to the Airport. When we arrived I paid the driver and headed for the British Airlines counter. I still had the return tickets to London and the continuing flight to California, though I figured they were considerably out of date by now.

"You're a bit early," said the ticket agent. "These tickets are for tomorrow's flight."

"What? That can't be. We've been in Greece for several weeks."

"Not according to our information," she said looking at the computer monitor. "You've been in Greece just over a week."

By this time almost nothing surprised me. After living for what seemed like months back in 430 B.C. it was a mild shock to learn that our adventures had been compressed into just about a week. I suppose it made little difference, but I was now more disoriented than ever.

"Okay," I said, "we'll be back tomorrow for our flight to London; but right now we'd like to change our flight from there to San Francisco, rather than Los Angeles."

"I'll see if I can do that," said the ticket agent.

Several minutes later she gave me the good news as she printed the new tickets. We would now *return to the place you first loved*, as the Oracle at Delphi proclaimed. I figured what have we got to lose? If the Oracle insisted that was the way to fall in love again, it was simply adding insurance to our already improved relationship, and that was good enough for me.

I turned to tell Lisa the happy news. We would soon be in San Francisco, our favorite city and the place we fell in love. But she was not there. I couldn't believe she would wander off without a word. Could she possibly be searching for another flush toilet? I asked the agent if she knew what happened to my wife.

"No," she said, "but I noticed she was speaking with two men while we were discussing your travel plans."

"Two men? Were they heavyset, like bodyguards?"

"Now that you mention it, they were."

Oh no, I thought. I cannot believe this is happening.

While I remained there, not knowing what to do, I asked the agent if I might charge my phone while I waited.

"There's a charging station right over there," she answered.

Twenty minutes later my phone was charged, but there was still no Lisa. I began to fear the worst possible scenario. I was certain Hades' thugs had abducted her, but I heard no sound, not a scream, not a peep. If she was kidnapped, however, I was facing another hazardous adventure. Honest to God, this was too much. After all we'd been through I needed another crisis like I needed another spear in the arm.

TWENTY-ONE

My initial thought, regarding Lisa's disappearance, was to notify the police. But what would I tell them? What kind of a story would make sense?

You see, officer, we were, standing at the ticket counter when my wife was suddenly abducted by a couple of beefy guys in black suits. One minute they were here, and then they were gone—and so was my wife. I'm positive those guys were working for Hades. Hades who, you ask? You know, the ancient Greek god of the underworld; the one who lives among the dead, with his wife, Persephone—that's the Hades I'm talking about. If you put out an all-points-bulletin you should know he has a thick beard, wears a full-length tunic, and carries a long wooden staff. And by the way, he's often seen with a three-headed dog named Cerberus. You can't miss him.

I figured they'd have me locked up in a psychiatric ward before the echo of my words faded away. No, contacting the police was not the answer. While I was ruminating about my next move I looked up and spotted Alexandros. He was walking through the airport looking in all directions.

"Alexandros," I called. He turned, looked my way, and walked quickly in my direction.

"I've been looking for you everywhere," he said. "And by the way, where's your wife?"

"That's what I'd like to know. I suspect she's been kidnapped by those men you spoke to at the highway rest stop."

"Oh, bad luck! I knew they were trouble when they first approached me, and I was certain they intended to do you harm. What did you do to provoke them?"

"It's a long story that involves their boss, the man who sent them here."

"Do you owe him money?"

"No, it's nothing like that. It's more complicated and far more serious."

"When they asked if I had seen you," said Alexandros, "I said I took you to the train station an hour ago. I told them you were headed to Paris on the Orient Express. I figured that would throw them off course. They insisted I drive them to the same station; that is why we drove off without telling you. I realized you would feel abandoned, but I had no other way to protect you. I am sorry to be a disappointment once again"

"You did the right thing, Alexandros, and I am grateful for your quick thinking. But how did they even know we were at the rest stop?"

"I don't think they did know. All they knew is that you were on the road to the airport, so they took a taxi from Athens intending to stop at every highway rest stop along the way and ask if anyone had seen you two. They found the place all right, but fortunately for you, they didn't bother to check the snack bar. I suspect they're not very bright."

"That's probably true, but they make up for their dim wits with incredible determination."

"After I took them to the train station," continued Alexandros, "I came back to the airport, since I figured you'd eventually be here. They may have followed me; I don't know."

"So what do we do now?" I asked.

Alexandros was quiet for a while before he said, "I have an idea where they may be. They mentioned the Grande Bretagne Hotel. That is where *you* stayed, is it not?"

"Well, that's the place we had reservations; but that, too, is a long story."

"Why don't we go there now and check it out," suggested Alexandros.

While driving back to the city I became irritated knowing that Hades' henchmen were staying at one of the most expensive hotels in Athens. Everyone knew Hades was the most affluent of all gods, since the entire wealth of the earth was within his realm. But why, I wondered, would he use his wealth and power to chase two harmless Americans all the way back to the modern world? You had to assume he was pathologically hell-bent on getting revenge. What a spiteful fool!

I suddenly thought about Lisa. Who knew where she was and what might be happening to her at this very moment?

"Step on it," I said. "I'm really worried about Lisa." The limo was doing 135 kilometers per hour—nearly 85 miles an hour—a speed likely to attract the highway patrol, but at the moment, finding Lisa was my prime concern. We arrived at the Grande Bretagne twenty minutes later, and I went directly to the front desk.

"I'm looking for two large men who are staying here," I said. "They probably returned within the last hour and may have been accompanied by an attractive young woman. Do you remember seeing them?"

"I think I know the people you are referring to," said the clerk. "The two large men were practically carrying the young woman. She appeared to be drunk and was barely conscious."

"More likely she was drugged," I said. "Can you tell me their room number?"

"I'm sorry, sir, I'm not permitted to give out that information."

"This may be a matter of life and death," I pleaded.

"Shall I notify the police?"

"For the moment, I'd prefer to keep the police out of it."

I needed time to think; time to figure out what I would do if I *had* the room number. I couldn't very well barge in, wave hi, pick up my wife, and waltz out. Those two goons were probably waiting for me to try a daring rescue, and when I did they'd lower the boom. I could even imagine the headline in tomorrow's newspaper.

AMERICAN ARCHITECT AND WIFE FOUND STRANGLED IN LUXURY HOTEL
Foul play emanating from ancient underworld suspected

Alexandros came to the rescue. "I doubt that they'll leave the hotel while your wife is with them," he said, "so they'll probably order room service. I have a friend here who works in the kitchen. When they order some food you and I can pretend to be waiters and deliver it to them. Once inside, we can figure out our next move."

Figure out our next move? What was he thinking? Storming a hornet's nest without a plan would be suicidal.

"I like the idea," I said, "but here's what worries me. They know what we look like, so the moment we appear, even if we're dressed like waiters, they'll be ready for a battle."

"So we'll wear a disguise," said Alexandros. Life seemed so simple for my new collaborator. I actually thought the idea was pretty good, but I feared this might come off more like a wacky comedy than a serious sting operation. And we couldn't afford to play it for laughs; too much was at stake.

"Okay," said Alexandros, "let me speak to my friend; then we will make a plan."

He proceeded to the hotel kitchen, and I took a seat in the hotel's elegant reception area. I was seated next to a large potted palm so I could immediately duck behind it if one of the thugs happened to come downstairs. Five minutes later, the unlikely actually happened. A very large man came out of the elevator, dropped his key at the front desk, and left the hotel. He was substantially overweight and wore an ill-fitting black suit that appeared several years out of date. He also sported a haircut more dreadful than a Korean dictator's.

He looks like a Russian diplomat from the 1960s, I thought, but I'll bet he's one of Hades' boys. I walked to the front desk, where the clerk was in serious conversation with an older woman. I moved close enough to the key to read the room number—438. Then I returned to my seat and waited for Alexandros to return.

"I think I found their room," he said.

"Is it 438?" I asked.

"How did you know?"

"I did a little detective work of my own. Incidentally, one of the thugs just left the building."

"Then this would be a good time to strike," Alexandros suggested.

"He might return any moment," I said. "Perhaps he just went out for a breath of air."

"Still, fighting one thug is easier than two. Let's get some waiter outfits, put on disguises, and deliver some food to room 438. This should be easy."

I recalled hearing that phrase several times in the past, and never once—not even in my wildest dreams—was the result ever "easy". Nevertheless, sensing the danger Lisa must be feeling, I knew time was of the essence. And with one henchman gone this was probably our best opportunity. We went to the kitchen and Alexandros introduced me to his friend, an assistant chef named Stavros. "Try these on," he said. We put on the long aprons, jaunty hats, and white gloves. Then he got out some water-based paint and decorated our faces with heavy eyebrows and full moustaches. I looked in the mirror and was stunned to see a Grouch Marx impersonator staring back at me. I only hoped the thug upstairs would not fall down laughing before concluding our business.

We went up in the service elevator, walked down the hall, and knocked on the door. It took two more knocks before a voice asked, "Who's there?"

"Room Service."

"I didn't order anything from Room Service."

"Perhaps your companion did," I answered.

The door opened a crack and I could see the thug was wearing one of the hotel's guest robes and little more. "What did you bring?" he asked, warming to the idea of the unexpected meal.

"A tureen of avgolemono soup, moussaka, and assorted baklava and chocolates."

The door opened wider, and we rolled in the service cart. The suite was large and elegant, but Lisa was nowhere to be seen. She must be in the adjoining room, I thought.

"Put the cart near the window," ordered the thug.

Alexandros set up the table, placed the glasses, silverware, and napkin appropriately, and drew up a chair for Hades' henchman. After the thug was seated, Alexandros picked up the steaming tureen of what was essentially hearty chicken soup and carried it toward the unsuspecting diner. Just before reaching the table Alexandros appeared to trip, and the entire boiling tureen of soup ended up in the thug's lap.

He leaped from the table shouting, "Holy Hades! My lap is on fire! You clumsy idiot!"

"Quick, to the bathroom," said Alexandros, "I will turn on the shower."

The thug limped into the bathroom, and Alexandros quickly followed. That gave me the chance to open the bedroom door. As I suspected, there was Lisa lying on the bed with hands and feet tied and tape across her mouth. I quickly removed the tape.

"Who are you?" she cried. "And what do you want?"

"It's me," I replied, "You husband. I've come to rescue you."

"Thank God! But why the Groucho Marx get-up?"

"I'll explain everything later," I said.

I picked up Lisa, put her over my shoulder, and raced out of the room. I ran to the open service elevator, flipped a switch, pushed a button, and the door began to close. At that very moment I saw across the hall the door of a passenger elevator opening. Thug Number One was stepping out of the car. "Hurry!" I shouted into the hall. "There's been an accident!"

Meanwhile, I noticed Alexandros running like a gazelle for the stairway. By the time we reached the ground floor he was already in the kitchen.

"Quick," I said to Stavros, "I need a knife for the rope." When Lisa was free, we fell into each other's arms. "No time for that," said Alexandros. "We must leave at once!"

We raced to the employee's parking lot, jumped into Alexandros' limousine, and sped away.

"We did it!" shouted our joyous driver. "We fooled that thickheaded hoodlum and gave him a burning crotch he will never forget!"

"Tell me," I asked, "where did you get that deft move with the boiling tureen?"

"Oh that; it's one of the first things you learn in Clown School."

"Clown School? You went to Clown School?"

"Yes, but I changed my mind once I began driving a limousine. I was not cut out for show business, and I truly find more pleasure driving an elegant car around town."

I sat in the back seat with Lisa cradled in my arms, and I gave her a loving kiss.

"You've really got to stop getting kidnapped," I said. "Rescuing you is putting a terrible strain on this relationship."

"I know," she said, "most people go through life without ever getting kidnapped, but I can't seem to get through a week without an incident. As for you, George, thanks once again; you will always be my hero."

We were racing through town on side streets, as Alexandros insisted it was best to avoid the main boulevards. "I am taking you to a friend's apartment," he said. "Hades' henchmen may try to find my place, and I don't want you exposed to any more danger. I think you will be comfortable for the night. Tomorrow morning I will pick you up and take you to the airport."

"You are a true friend," I said, "and we will never forget what you've done for us."

"I just want you to know," he said, "some Greeks can be trusted."

TWENTY-TWO

Alexandros' friend was a struggling artist named Panos. He was a handsome young man whose best features appeared to derive from the Greek gods themselves. His paintings, which covered most walls of the small studio, showed remarkable talent. His specialty appeared to be portraiture, and by some eerie coincidence, he was currently doing a series of portraits of ancient Greek gods. Many of their features were abstracted, yet most were recognizable as the familiar faces we saw during our recent visit to the *old world*, as I now thought of it. The heads of Aphrodite, Hermes, Persephone, Ares, and our latest nemesis, Hades were all there, life size, and staring at us from every wall.

"These are terrific," I said. "And you've captured the personalities as well as the likenesses. Tell me, how did you know what they looked like?"

"For some time now," he said, "I studied ancient myths and likenesses others have painted or sculpted through the ages. That's how I came up with my own interpretations. Since no one knows exactly what they looked like, these are probably as accurate as one could imagine."

"For the most part you're right," I said, "but some features could be rendered more accurately. For example, your portrait of Aphrodite is beautiful, but you made the same mistake Botticelli made in his *Birth of Venus*. Her mouth is somewhat wider, and the chin is less prominent.

As for Hermes, your painting is quite accurate, except for the hair. His is far more ample and curlier than you've indicated."

"How do you know these things?" asked Panos.

"I just do," I answered. "You must trust me."

"My husband is right," added Lisa. "You should believe what he tells you."

"How about Ares?" asked Panos warily. "Any opinion about that painting?"

"You have captured his personality appropriately," I said. "But you could have made those eyebrows a bit heavier. That would truly capture his generally malevolent expression."

Panos appeared baffled by what he heard. I'm sure he thought we were being oddly critical, if not actually a bit deranged, but he was cordial enough to let the matter drop. He said, "I will consider your comments, and I thank you for those insights."

Alexandros' friend was an affable host, and that evening he prepared a simple dinner of cold foods, which we enjoyed while sitting around a small table at one end of the studio. We remained there drinking wine and chatting for another hour before I noticed Lisa yawning.

"Perhaps we should call it a day," I suggested. "The last twenty-four hours has been unbelievably hectic."

Panos led us to a narrow convertible sofa that was to be our bed for the night. It may have been small, but it was our first bed in weeks that didn't feature a mattress filled with dried leaves. After the extraordinary events of the day Lisa and I slept that night as if drugged.

When we awoke, the pungent aroma of brewing coffee filled the small studio.

"Your ride to the airport will be here soon," said Panos.

"We'll be ready to go in another minute or two," I replied. "There's no packing to do."

Alexandros arrived fifteen minutes later, and we all had coffee and rolls that Panos had purchased earlier that morning at the local bakery.

"We want to thank you for your hospitality," I said. "You have made our final evening in Greece a genuine pleasure, and we are grateful."

"It was nice to meet you," said Panos. "I hope your travels go smoothly and safely."

We shook hands, said goodbye, and sped away to the airport. A half hour later, as we neared the British Air terminal, I was shocked to see Thug Number One standing outside. He apparently knew about our flight to London.

"Stop here," I said; "Hades' henchman is directly in front of the entrance."

"I have an idea," said Alexandros. "Get out here and walk the rest of the way. In a moment I plan to divert our plump friend. When the distraction begins, go to the front desk and check in. For now, I say goodbye and may the gods carry you safely home."

As he stepped out of the car we hugged, shook hands, and I thanked him for his help. "I hope we meet again," I said, "and until we do, you have our everlasting gratitude."

We strolled towards the terminal as Alexandros guided the car directly towards the henchman. As he came close to the entrance he gunned the engine, blasted the horn, and drove right up and over the curb onto the sidewalk. The thug jumped out of the way and began to run away from the terminal. All the while Alexandros continued blowing the car's horn and creating a monstrous distraction.

Lisa and I ran into the terminal as most others were running out to see what the commotion was about. We raced to the ticket counter and presented our passports.

"Have you any luggage to check?" asked the agent.

"No," was the reply.

"Any cabin bags?" Another no.

"So, you're traveling to London without anything?" she asked incredulously.

"We're traveling very light," I answered.

The agent gave us a quizzical look but immediately directed us to the security checkpoint.

As I looked back outside I noticed that Alexandros was standing near his limousine and the thug was shaking a fist at him. By this time airport police, attracted by the noisy commotion, surrounded them both. Somehow I knew Alexandros would emerge victorious. After all, his basic training was at Clown School, and I suspected clowns could survive any bizarre predicament.

After passing through security we proceeded to the First Class lounge. Our flight was scheduled to leave in forty minutes, and we decided to spend that time having a drink, relaxing, and reading a newspaper. I had not read a paper in weeks and had no idea what in the world was going on. As it turned out, little had changed. They were still rioting in Africa and practically everywhere else on earth, for that matter.

Just before our flight was ready to board I was stunned to see Thug Number One enter the lounge. He approached and asked, "Going somewhere?"

"Indeed we are, so stand aside, Butterball. By the way, how did you get in here?"

"The same way you did; I bought a ticket."

"It must be nice having an unlimited expense account."

He ignored the comment and said, "I believe we have some unfinished business."

"I don't think so. We're through with you, so why don't you get lost."

"Not so fast; I have a job to do, and I intend to do it."

"You really wouldn't make a scene in a first class lounge, would you?"

"I have no intention of making a scene here." The thug was no longer smiling; his expression turned malicious as he grabbed my arm and said, "Come with me to the men's room where we can have some privacy."

"Look, pal, this whole revenge thing is getting annoying. You have no reason to dislike me. You're just doing a dirty job because Hades is paying you. Why don't we call it off? You can tell your boss you messed me up, and he'll never know the difference. What do you say?"

"I say be quiet and come with me."

I suddenly pointed in the other direction and said, "Oh my God, what's going on over there?" He released his grip on my arm, and as he turned to look I quickly picked up two packets of sugar from the snack counter and slipped them into his coat pocket.

"I don't see anything," he said.

"Sorry, my mistake. Excuse me for a second, I forgot something."

He followed me as I headed to the front desk and said to the admitting agent, "Call the authorities immediately. This man just offered to sell me cocaine! And be careful, he may be armed."

The agent grabbed a phone, and before the henchman could possibly realize what was happening two airport police officers walked through the door. "What's going on?" they wanted to know.

I repeated my accusation, and the confused thug had the most perplexed look I'd ever seen.

"This is preposterous!" he cried. "I am a respectable businessman; I have no time for such nonsense. This man is making crazy accusations."

"Check his coat pockets," I suggested. "And while you're at it, check to see if he's armed."

One of the officers discovered the two packets of sugar I planted just moments ago, in addition to a small handgun tucked into an ankle holster. "What's all this?" he asked.

"It looks like sugar," said the suddenly nervous thug.

"What's it doing in your coat pocket?" asked the officer.

"I had no idea it was there," he answered.

"That's the same stuff he tried to sell me," I said. "If I were you, I'd take it to the lab and find out what it really is."

"And the gun?" asked the officer. "What about that?"

"I have enemies, so I carry protection."

"How did you get through security with your 'protection'?"

"They must have missed that," he answered.

"I think you better come with us," said the officer.

"But I'll miss my flight," said the thug. His voice was suddenly an octave higher, and his hands began to shake uncontrollably.

"You can catch another flight tomorrow," suggested the officer, "if you're still a free man."

The thug glowered at me as he was led away, and I said to him, "Give my regards to you buddy, and be sure to thank Hades for the use of his chariot." Both officers gave me a totally bewildered look.

"Let's go to England," I said to Lisa. We boarded the plane, settled into our comfortable seats, and enjoyed the next four hours of peace and relative silence. I believe to this day that one of the greatest benefits of flying six miles above the earth is the realization that, for the length of the flight, your life is in the hands of experienced professionals who have your safety and comfort uppermost in mind. There is nothing expected of you; your total responsibility is to sit quietly and enjoy views of the clouds below. It's like being an infant again; one is fed, entertained, and pampered by people whose only interest is your well-being.

A light rain was falling when we arrived in London, but even a typhoon could not have dampened our spirits. We had now returned to one of the most civilized spots on earth.

"How wonderful to be back," said Lisa, as we returned to the Savoy Hotel. "I'm going to take a long shower, put on a fluffy robe, and take a short nap. Hope you don't mind, George."

"Hope *you* don't mind if I join you in the shower, put on *my* robe, and hop in bed with you."

"What a wonderful idea," she said.

We arose early in the afternoon, asked our concierge to make an appointment with an obstetrician for later that afternoon, and enjoyed a delicious lunch in the dining room. The doctor we saw was young, but he immediately put us at ease with his genial manner and cheerful style. It took only fifteen minutes to confirm what we already knew—Lisa was indeed pregnant. And by the doctor's rough calculation the baby would appear in about eight months.

After reviewing her health history and performing a superficial exam he said, "You appear to be in good health, and your pregnancy should be free from most problems associated with this experience. You may, on the other hand, have some fatigue, headaches, and possible nausea. But if you take care of yourself and watch you diet you should avoid major complications. My advice is to avoid smoking, excessive drinking, and riding in the next Royal Ascot at Epson." Then he chuckled at his own little joke.

We thanked the doctor, practically skipped out of the office, and set out to buy some new clothes at Harrods in Knightsbridge. We also bought a small suitcase to carry our purchases and to avoid the embarrassment of traveling to California like homeless gypsies.

Over dinner that night Lisa glowed with the delight of knowing we would become parents. "This is a special day," she said, "and a day I've waited for all my life."

Then she asked, "Do you think we're really through with ancient Greece?" She looked worried; as if she thought some mythological creature would suddenly pop out of a potted plant and upset our life.

"I can't say for sure, but I believe our once-in-a-lifetime experience is over. I'm sure it's something we will never forget, and something we will eventually tell our child about. Whether or not he chooses to believe us, it will always be a part of this family's history."

TWENTY-THREE

We returned to Heathrow the next morning and caught our transatlantic flight to San Francisco. The trip was long, but uneventful. We landed in the early afternoon and went by taxi to our hotel near Fisherman's Wharf.

"This is it," I said. "The place I still dream about, and the location the Oracle had in mind when she said, *Return to the place you first loved.*"

"Such memories!" said Lisa. "I will never forget this place or that night. And here we are, back where it all began."

We settled into our room and decided to take a nap before having dinner. We planned to have the same dinner we enjoyed that night we fell in love. We both recalled it was freshly caught cracked crab, accompanied by that incredible San Francisco sour dough bread and a Napa Valley Sauvignon Blanc to wash it all down. I can almost taste it now, as I recall that delightful meal.

After our recent time in ancient Athens, where we faced a frightening array of dangers, I had become more than a bit paranoid. I'd always been aware of what was going on around me, but now I felt exceptionally sensitive to nearly everything surrounding us. As we walked to the Wharf that evening the weather turned chilly and a thick fog began to roll in off the bay. If one were to conceive the perfect setting for a murder mystery, that location on that evening would have been it.

I suddenly had the uncomfortable feeling we were being followed. I was not aware of footsteps or voices or anything unusual in the passing traffic; I just sensed something ominous. I paused and said, "Let's slow down and look at the shop windows." This gave me a chance to look back to verify my suspicions. No one was behind us, nor did anyone on either side of the street show the slightest interest in us. I began to feel my paranoia was out of control. *Get a grip*, I thought. But try as I might, I couldn't shake the feeling that something unpleasant was still out there.

We arrived at our favorite restaurant on the Wharf, and the maitre d' led us to a comfortable booth overlooking the colorful fishing boats bobbing peacefully in the water.

"Let's start with a martini," suggested Lisa. "It will be like old times."

We sat quietly sipping our drinks and absorbing the view, the sounds, and the aromas of our bayside perch. It was incredibly nostalgic. Then Lisa said, "After all we've been through, the good times and the bad, I want you to know, George, that at this very moment I love you more than ever and more than I thought possible."

I was so touched by her words my eyes began to fill with tears. Finally I said, "Thanks for saying that, Lisa; it means a lot to me. But if it happens to be the martini talking, let's have another."

"It's not the drink, silly boy; it's you. It really is you."

A short time later Lisa got up and said, "I'll be right back. Have to fix my makeup."

I stared at her disappearing figure and thought: *I am surely the luckiest guy in the world to be married to such a desirable woman.*

After fifteen minutes passed and Lisa had not returned, I called a waitress and asked if she would kindly check the Lady's Room to be sure Lisa was all right. I was beginning to worry, as those ominous feelings returned.

The waitress came back a moment later and said, "There's no one in the Lady's Room, sir. I checked the stalls and they're empty."

I was upset, but not surprised. I jumped up and ran to the Lady's Room to see for myself. I barged into the room without knocking, scared one old lady half to death, and confirmed that no one else was there. Then I paid for the drinks, ran back to our hotel and checked our room. Everything was exactly as we left it.

Oh no, I thought, not again. Honest to God, this is really too much. I had no doubt that someone or something from ancient Greece was still pursuing us. Damn it all to hell, I thought, why don't they give it up and leave us alone?

I sat in our room considering my options. We were now back in the U.S., a country that operated under the rule of law. I knew I should contact the police; I had to report Lisa missing. I made the call, and three minutes later there was a knock on the door. I opened it and a large uniformed person said, "I'm Detective Haddas. What seems to be the trouble? He spoke with a strong accent.

"My wife is missing," I said. "I believe she's been abducted. But how did you get here so quickly? I only reported her missing a moment ago."

"I was in the vicinity when the report came in. When did you notice she was missing?"

"Not even half an hour ago. We were at a restaurant on the Wharf, and she went to the Lady's Room. That was the last I saw of her."

"Was there trouble between you two?"

"No! Definitely not! We were celebrating an anniversary. We were happy to be together. Are you suggesting she left of her own free will without saying goodbye?"

"Stranger things have happened."

"Well, I think she's been kidnapped. She would never leave without a word. We were sitting quietly having a drink; we hadn't even ordered dinner."

"Do you have any enemies, anyone who might want to do you harm?" he asked.

How could I possibly tell him about ancient Greece; about the conflicts we had at one time or another with Ares, Hermes, or Hades, not to mention half the Spartan army? Those stories would be a one-way ticket to the loony bin. So I said, "Not that I know of."

"Are you sure?" asked the Detective. He seemed curiously suspicious.

"Yes, I'm sure."

"You're a visitor here, are you not?"

"That's right."

"Where did you come from most recently?"

"London."

"And before that?"

"What are you driving at?"

"Did you visit other places? There may be a clue in where you've recently been."

"We spent some time in Athens."

"I see," said the Detective. "Very interesting."

"Why interesting?" I asked.

Before he could answer, there was a knock on the door and I went to open it. Standing in the doorway was an older gentleman with a full head of white hair and well-trimmed beard. He was dressed in a three-piece tweed suit and colorful bow tie. He had a pleasant smile as he introduced himself. "I am Inspector Zunas, and I'm here to speak to you about your missing wife."

"Come in Inspector. This is Detective Haddas. He, too, is here about my wife."

"Yes," said the Inspector, "he and I have met before." They nodded at each another.

"Is there something about my wife's disappearance that particularly interests the San Francisco Police Department?" I asked. "It seems the response to my call was incredibly swift, and now there's a Detective *and* an Inspector involved in the investigation. What's going on?"

There was a long silence before either of them spoke. "Shall I tell him?" the Inspector finally asked, "or will you?"

"Tell me what?" The conversation was becoming disconcerting.

"To begin with," began the Inspector, "neither of us works for the San Francisco Police Department. We intercepted your phone call before it reached the police."

I was totally bewildered and said so. "Then who in the hell are you two, and what interest do you have in me? More importantly, has this anything to do with my missing wife?"

The Inspector said, "Please sit down and I will explain what is going on."

I sat on the edge of the bed and said, "Okay, let's have it; I want the whole story."

"I am not actually Inspector Zunas," he began. "That is a convenient alias I often assume when away from home. I am better known as Zeus, ruler of Mount Olympus, deity of the heavens, and king of all gods.

"Hole shit," I said. I was absolutely stunned. "What on earth are *you* doing here?"

"Allow me to continue. My associate, Detective Haddas, is also in disguise. He is actually your persistent nemesis, Hades. He happens to be my brother, as well as supreme god of the underworld. You did not recognize him because he shaved his beard and is wearing a modern uniform, but his accent might have been a clue."

I sat there in stunned silence before finally saying to Hades, "So, you are the infamous god of the underworld who continues to pursue us. Do you happen to know where my wife might be?"

"First, allow me to explain my interest in you," he replied. "I am here to seek revenge, nothing more or less. We have a strict rule in the underworld: all are welcome, dead or alive, but none are permitted to leave. No one—ever! A few have broken that rule in the past, but none had the unmitigated impudence or displayed such contempt to use my private chariot and horses. And the way you treated my associates in Athens was unforgivable. One is still in the hospital, and the other is in jail for a crime he did not commit. Those actions engendered the antagonism I now feel for you. My holy mission remains this: I wish to cause you the same pain and discomfort you have caused me."

"So you kidnapped my wife for revenge? Is that what I understand?"

"Yes, that is absolutely correct."

"If you understood the reason we escaped with the help of your horses and chariot you might better understand that our prime motive was to return to the land of the living. It had nothing to do with contempt for you, nor was it meant to cause you distress. Your charming wife, Persephone, assured us we would have no problem returning from the underworld. Had we believed otherwise we never would have attempted the trip in the first place. Furthermore, what loss did you actually suffer? Where's the damage? I understand your feelings are hurt, but the only injury, it seems, was to your vanity. Finally, you should realize that revenge is unworthy of a powerful god such as you. It is a dreadful disease that devours the soul and breeds hate in the heart. A desire for retribution may be understandable, but you must remember that *an eye for an eye* leaves everybody blind. Be angry, if you must, but forgive, forget, and get on with your life."

"Well spoken," said Zeus. "Perhaps that will change my brother's addled mind. Incidentally, you should know that I am here for one reason alone, and that is to persuade Hades to give up this vendetta against you and your wife. Too much time and energy have been wasted on this foolish escapade, and there are far more important matters to deal with at home. I hope he will agree to return to the underworld where he belongs and pursue his rightful duties. If, on the other hand, he persists in his campaign of terror against you I shall use every power I possess to make certain he will never again bother you. This feud must end, and it must end now!"

"My dear brother forgets," said Hades, "that he is god of the heavens and I am the god of the underworld. Since we both share the earth's realm he has no power over me when we are here."

"Quite the contrary, Hades. You, above all others, should know that I am the king of all gods, and whether in heaven or the underworld, on earth or seas, my word is supreme! You will do as I say, or else . . ."

I began to feel genuine fear as the two gods bickered over Lisa and me. Was I about to witness an epic battle of wills? I wanted no part of this titanic struggle. So I said, "Gentlemen, allow me to offer another thought. My wife and I have become insignificant pawns in a battle that is not worth fighting. I wish to apologize to you, Hades. We never meant you harm or discomfort. You have already reaped the satisfaction of driving us crazy. Isn't that enough? Let us be done with this nonsense and move on to more important matters. We shall return home, you shall return to Greece, and with luck, we shall never meet again. And now please tell me, where is my wife?"

The two gods began to speak to each other in low voices. I could only guess by their posture that a battle to the death had been avoided. Moments later Zeus said, "Hades has agreed to accept your apology and put this matter to rest. Now, as to your wife, she will return here shortly. She is safe and has been treated well. Her abduction was never meant to do her harm; it was only meant—as you put it—to drive you crazy. So our business is done, and we bid you goodbye."

"My gratitude to you both," I said. "It has been an honor to meet you, and I wish you smooth sailing for all your immortal years." And then they were gone without another word. I was finally convinced I would never see either of them again.

Twenty minutes later Lisa walked into our hotel room. We embraced in silence and clung to each other as though we had been apart for years.

"Are you okay?" I asked.

"I am now," she answered.

We remained in each other's arms until I asked, "Care for some dinner?"

"Sure," she said, "let's go back to the Wharf and finish what we started."

Over our late dinner that night I recounted the details of my meeting with Hades and Zeus. "It was all about revenge. Our escape from the underworld badly bruised Hades' ego. And stealing his chariot and horses drove him over the edge. It damaged his pride and was more that he could handle. So he decided to punish us. He was trying to show us that there is a price to pay when you mess with a powerful god. Were it not for Zeus's intervention I'm sure he'd still be making our life miserable. But it's finally over now, and I truly believe there is nothing more to worry about."

"That's the best news I've heard in a long time," said Lisa.

We finished our dinner, strolled back to our hotel, and fell into bed. It had been an adventurous day and we were exhausted. We fell into a deep sleep, still in each other's arms.

The following day we flew home to Los Angeles. We had been gone almost two weeks, but it felt like a lifetime had passed. Before long we were back at work, seeing family and friends, and picking up the life we abandoned weeks earlier. The difference, however, was that we were expecting a baby in several months and, like long ago, we were more in love than ever.

It would take time to put our trip to ancient Greece in perspective, but time is what we had plenty of. Some day, I thought, this adventure will be a part of our past, but right now we needed to think about it, savor it, and digest it.

Twenty-Four

Eleven years has passed since our return from ancient Greece. We remain in the same house in the same neighborhood of the same city, but we are now a family of three. Our bright young son, Samuel Socrates Newman recently celebrated his tenth birthday, and in every way he makes us proud. He is clever, charming, and very good-looking. That should come as no surprise, considering the natural beauty of his mother. Over the past few years Lisa remains virtually unchanged. She is still the most appealing woman I have ever known.

Sam goes to public school, where his grades are well above average. He is popular with students and teachers alike, and his closest friends call him by the initials S.S., as in the seagoing vessel, S.S. Newman. I often ask how things are going at school, and like most boys his age his one word answer is, "Good."

"Anything you'd like to talk about?" I ask.

"Nope."

"You know, when I was your age I had plenty of things on my mind."

"So?"

"So I was wondering if you had anything on your mind that I could help you with."

"Like what?"

"Like anything you might want to discuss."

"Nope. Thanks anyway."

Old friends enjoy speaking to Sam, since he has the sensibility of a wise old man. You can engage him on nearly any subject, and you will find he holds strong opinions on nearly every one. An associate of mine recently asked him if he planned to become an architect, like his father.

"I don't think so," he said. "Not that there's anything wrong with being an architect, you know, but I'm more interested in philosophy." The kid is only ten, and his interest in philosophy baffles everyone, except Lisa and me. We alone know from where the inspiration derives.

Lisa suggested we start saving our money so that Sam will have a sizable inheritance. "It's pretty clear he's going to need help," she said. "Philosophers *never* make a living."

"He's only ten," I pointed out. "He has no idea what the world is about. Next year he might want to be a baseball player, an astronaut, or a brain surgeon. Who knows?"

"All I know is this," said Lisa. "He already *is* a philosopher."

So I was surprised one day when my philosopher son, Samuel Socrates Newman, asked if I had a moment to speak to him.

"Sure, son, what's on your mind?"

"I met this lady outside of school," he said. "She's been there before but she never spoke to me. She just stands there and looks at me, and mostly she smiles. She's really pretty. Well, anyway, yesterday she spoke to me. She introduced herself and said she was my goddess mother. I know godmothers are people who are responsible for little kids, but I never heard of a goddess mother. Do you know what that is?"

When Lisa and I returned from our extraordinary adventure several years before, we decided not to reveal our bizarre experiences to anyone. What would be the point? They would think that either we fabricated the entire story or that we had lost our minds. And who needed that? That's why I was sure the appearance of Sam's goddess was not a prank.

Nobody had any idea we visited ancient Greece, nor could anyone possibly guess we met a goddess. I suddenly felt apprehensive. This had to be someone from our ancient past—someone I was certain we would never see again.

"I really don't know who that person could be," I said, "but I'll look into it and we'll figure it out." I hoped my answer would satisfy him for the moment.

That evening I told Lisa about Sam's visitor. "I suspect Aphrodite is in Los Angeles," I said, "and it sounds irrational even saying those words."

"What could she possibly want?" asked Lisa.

"Well obviously, to see Sam."

"Do you think he's in any danger?"

"I hope not, but remember the story of her and Adonis? She became enamored of his beauty and had Persephone care for him in the underworld until he reached a suitable age. When he did, both goddesses fought for his romantic attention until Zeus got involved. He ordered them to stop quarrelling and learn to share his affection."

"You don't think Aphrodite has a sexual interest in our son, do you?"

"I certainly hope not, but why would she hang around the schoolyard like your typical, garden variety pervert?"

"What can we do?" asked Lisa. She was taking this potential threat as seriously as I.

"What we *can't* do is involve the authorities," I said. "Can you imagine what they'd do if I told them an ancient Greek goddess had designs on our ten-year-old son? Good God, they'd put the kid in a foster home and lock up his parents in a maximum security nut house."

"So what *can* we do?"

"I'll try to intercept her at school and find out what this is all about."

The following afternoon I parked across the street from the school entrance, where I had a view of the students as they were exiting. I watched carefully as they left the building and saw Sam begin to walk home with a couple of friends. Aphrodite did not appear. I did the same thing the next day, and again, no Aphrodite. Could she have recognized me and was now avoiding contact? Or could Sam have fabricated the story to get attention? That seemed extremely unlikely.

Finally, on the third day, I spotted Aphrodite. She was dressed in fashionably modern clothes, but there was no disguising her remarkable beauty. She was absolutely radiant. Standing near the exit door she could see the children pass by when school was out. I got out of the car, walked across the street, and came up behind her. "Well, what a surprise this is," I said.

She turned, appeared startled, and said, "Why, George, how wonderful to see you again; it's been a long time. How nice you look; those little flecks of gray hair make you appear more attractive than ever."

"Thanks; you're not looking so bad yourself."

"Well, of course; I never change. I look the same as the day I emerged from the sea."

"I have to admit," I said, "I'm amazed to see you here; you're such a long way from home. Tell me, why *are* you here?"

"I was curious about you and your family. Since I was instrumental in resolving your problems, I wanted to see how everything turned out, including the child conceived in Greece."

"You wouldn't be meddling in our lives again, would you?"

"That sounds so negative, George. The last time I meddled in your life it turned out pretty well, wouldn't you agree? I mean, look at you, successful architect, loving wife, and beautiful son."

"About our son, what is your interest in him? He says you told him you were his goddess mother. What did you mean by that?"

"Well, a godmother feels responsible for a young person, and since I'm a goddess, I thought the term goddess mother would be more descriptive."

"With all due respect, our relationship ended in Greece. Our son is no longer your responsibility—or concern. Your presence here just adds unnecessary complications to our life."

"I must say, George, I didn't expect this kind of reception. I feel particularly unwelcome. After all I've done for you it's difficult to understand your reaction."

"Please try to understand, we will always be grateful for what you did for us. But we come from different worlds. We can never have a conventional relationship. You are a goddess, we are mortals; you are mythical, we are real; finally, you are eternal, but one day each of us will die. We are as different as night is from day and as Hellenic Greece is from the twenty-first century."

"But still we have much in common," said Aphrodite. "We share similar emotions; we love, we hate, we experience moods and passions, and we laugh and cry. Is that not true?" She seemed unable to accept that what we shared was not nearly as enduring as what divided us.

"I cannot argue with you," I said. "Much of what you say is true. And though you will always have our gratitude, we must finally say goodbye. We cannot live in the same century; you must return to your time and place."

"If that's the way you feel, George, I will do as you suggest." She appeared crushed by the rejection, as well as the realization that our relationship was simply unsustainable.

"You will never hear from me again," she said. "I must tell you, however, that I loved every moment we were together and every adventure we shared. I wish for you, Lisa, and your beautiful child a happy and loving life."

And then—just like that—she was gone. I don't know how that happened, but one moment she was there, and the next moment she wasn't. I assumed it was forever, and suddenly I felt tremendous guilt and sorrow. I knew I would never forget her and that the sadness would continue for years into the future.

"So what do you think she was doing here?" asked Lisa. I had just recounted my conversation with Aphrodite.

"I think she was curious about our family, just as she said. She seemed as fascinated with us as we were with her. As the goddess of love, she was strongly affected by the transformation of our relationship, something she herself engineered.

"And you believe she had no romantic fantasies about Sam—or quite possibly you?"

"Me? Are you serious?"

"You should know, George, women notice the way other women look at their husbands. I would think you'd be flattered. After all she is the goddess of love: she could have anyone."

"As a matter of fact," I said, "she practically *has* had everyone. That is, everyone but me. As for Sam, I think our imagination got carried away. Blame it on that myth about Adonis."

"So, you think we've seen the end of the ancient Greeks?" asked Lisa.

"I do; but my opinion doesn't come with any guarantees."

I spoke to Sam the following day and told him that I ran into the beautiful lady he met outside of school. "She was someone we met years ago when your mom and I traveled to Greece. We had not seen her since then, but she knew we had a son and she wanted to meet you."

"So what was that business about goddess mother?"

"That was a joke. She is so pretty we used to call her a goddess, and since she feels she knows you she thinks of herself as your godmother."

"Will we see her again?"

"Afraid not; she's already on her way home."

"What's her name?" asked Sam.

"Aphrodite," I said.

"Wasn't Aphrodite an ancient goddess?" My ten-year-old apparently knew everything.

"Yes," I said, "our friend was named after her. Quite appropriate, wouldn't you say?"

"I sure would. She was prettier than anyone I ever saw—except for mom, of course."

TWENTY-FIVE

We never again heard from Aphrodite, or for that matter, any other ancient Greek. After several months passed I was convinced we never would. As far as we were concerned the Hellenic adventure was over, and all that remained were the extraordinary memories. Most of those resembled a bizarre cocktail consisting of one part reality to nine parts improbability.

"Did it really happen?" Lisa asked one day. "I mean, what if our trip was only a fantasy, a fantasy we shared simultaneously? What do we really know for sure?"

"I've thought about that," I said, "but when I see the scar on my left arm—the one caused by a Spartan spear—I know it was not entirely a fantasy."

Early in life I learned to distinguish between what was real and what was not. Though I enjoyed fairy tales and magic tricks as much as the next person, I generally knew what was genuine and what was an illusion. Reality was provable; miracles were not. And what one believed to be true didn't really matter; only the truth mattered. So what *was* the truth?

First, Lisa and I were on the verge of ending a loving relationship. That much was clear. Secondly, my retarded sperm required a global positioning system that was medically unavailable. Lisa hated me for that, as well as for an unending list of perceived deficiencies. At the same time I was losing patience, and on many occasions, would have happily strangled her. So that was our situation before leaving home.

Happily—and somewhat inexplicably—all that changed during the time we spent in ancient Greece. We overcame our problems, reignited our love for one another, and conceived a wonderful child. So who really cares what part of our adventure was real and what part was mythical?

Myths are stories that were invented to explain the unexplainable. I'd be the last one in the world to disparage them, because I believe myths have a valuable function. They help people understand disturbing events like death and life after death. Some myths have been told and retold for years until they have become truths. That's how religion began, and that is how it continues today. And for the most part we love those myths, because reality is often difficult to handle. Some people have challenging lives; they work hard, grow old, and die in unpleasant ways. Who can blame them for believing in myths?

So my evolving philosophy comes down to this: Live and let live. Believe what you want to believe—myths, magic, miracles—it doesn't really matter. But if you want a happier world don't tell anyone else what to believe.

Lisa and I decided that some day we would tell our son about our experiences in ancient Greece. It would probably be well after he graduates from college with a Doctor of Philosophy degree and is teaching at some distinguished university. I doubt that he'll believe us, but at least the truth about his conception will be out there. And when he writes his first scholarly book, the brief biography on the inside will state that Professor Samuel Socrates Newman was conceived in ancient Athens, in the shadow of the Acropolis, by his devoted parents, to whom this book is lovingly dedicated—and for whom love did indeed find a way. And Lisa and I will be very proud.